"It's obvious that you love Henry dearly. All the love and care you've given matters. It's never too late for that to make a difference."

"I hope it does. He's had a hard young life. How did we get on this unpleasant subject?"

She gave him a thin-lipped smile. "Apparently, we both needed to talk. I'm glad you felt you could tell me."

Which wasn't like him. He was working hard to put what he could of his past in the past. "I think that's because you're easy to talk to."

"I'll take that as a compliment." She stood.

Chad did as well. "It was meant that way." He reached a hand out. "Henry, it's time to go in."

The boy came to him.

Chad brushed a finger along Izzy's jaw. "You do know it was his loss, don't you?"

Her eyes glistened. "That might be the nicest thing anyone has ever said to me." She gave him a quick kiss on the cheek. "Thank you."

Dear Reader,

A children's hospital is a special place with special people on staff and even more special patients. The doctors and nurses who work with sick children and their families have hearts and skills that surpass the norm. They are angels on earth. I know because I spent more than twenty years visiting and staying in a children's hospital with my youngest son, who has had a heart transplant.

In this story Izzy and Chad are the same type of people as those I knew from my son's hospital experiences. They work in the emergency department, where they listen, are passionate about their jobs and will do whatever necessary to take care of their patients. All these emotions spill over into their personal lives, making the sparks flying between them sharper and brighter.

I hope you enjoy the first of the Atlanta Children's Hospital series. I love to hear from my readers. You can reach me at www.susancarlisle.com.

Happy reading,

Susan

MENDING THE
ER DOC'S HEART

—

SUSAN CARLISLE

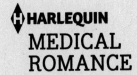

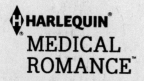

HARLEQUIN®
MEDICAL
ROMANCE™

Recycling programs
for this product may
not exist in your area.

ISBN-13: 978-1-335-73734-2

Mending the ER Doc's Heart

Copyright © 2022 by Susan Carlisle

For questions and comments about the quality of this book, please contact us at CustomerService@Harlequin.com.

Harlequin Enterprises ULC
22 Adelaide St. West, 41st Floor
Toronto, Ontario M5H 4E3, Canada
www.Harlequin.com

Printed in U.S.A.

Susan Carlisle's love affair with books began when she made a bad grade in mathematics. Not allowed to watch TV until the grade had improved, she filled her time with books. Turning her love of reading into a love for writing romance, she pens hot medicals. She loves castles, traveling, afternoon tea, reading voraciously and hearing from her readers. Join her newsletter at susancarlisle.com..

Books by Susan Carlisle

Harlequin Medical Romance

Miracles in the Making

The Neonatal Doc's Baby Surprise

First Response

Firefighter's Unexpected Fling

Pups that Make Miracles

Highland Doc's Christmas Rescue

Pacific Paradise, Second Chance
The Single Dad's Holiday Wish
Reunited with Her Daredevil Doc
Taming the Hot-Shot Doc
From Florida Fling to Forever

Visit the Author Profile page
at Harlequin.com for more titles.

To Josie, the granddaughter of my heart.
I love you!

**Praise for
Susan Carlisle**

"A wonderful, sweet, and enjoyable tale. Ms. Carlisle wrote a wonderful, flirty, and enjoyable romance that should not be missed. She provided a tale rich with emotions, sizzling chemistry, vivid scenic descriptions, and realistic characters…. I highly recommend *Pacific Paradise, Second Chance* to other readers."

—*Goodreads*

CHAPTER ONE

A CHILD'S SHRIEK ripped through the air at the other end of the grocery store aisle. Izzy Lane's heart jumped. The box of tea she'd touched fell to the floor, bringing down five others. Her head whipped toward the sound. What was going on? Was the child hurt?

As a pediatric nurse, that was always her first thought. Prepared to help, she looked down the aisle to see what the difficulty might be. No problem there. All she saw was a young boy of about three sitting in a cart, flailing his hands and kicking his feet until the cart rocked. As her heart rate returned to a regular pace, her concern turned to worry over the boy toppling the cart.

A tall solid-shouldered man wearing a knit golf shirt had his head down, talking to the child. "Shush, Henry. We talked about this before we came in."

The boy wailed, "I want Sugar Loops."

"You need to pick out another cereal." The man glanced at her, concern on his face, his mouth drawn into a tight line. Picking up a box, he showed the child. "What about these?"

"Sugar Loops!" the boy demanded at the top of his voice.

Izzy shook her head with a wry smile. It wasn't going well for the dad. She'd had her fair share of those moments in her line of work. Sometimes there were behavioral issues that weren't immediately obvious to others. Maybe that was the case here.

Her chest squeezed. She had to admit the boy was cute. With his cotton-white hair, full cheeks and big eyes. Despite his tantrum, Izzy wished she had a child who could give her a hard time. She'd believed that would happen with Richard until he'd cheated on her. For years he'd led her on, getting her to pay for his school by telling her he loved her. He had her believing he wanted to marry her and then start a family. Instead she'd just been used. Now that dream had been shattered.

Her attention returned to the jumble on the floor. The corner of her mouth lifted in exasperation. She had a mess to clean up. Setting her armload of items down, Izzy went to her knees and picked up the tea-bag boxes replacing them on the shelf.

Another yell vibrated around her. Izzy shuttered and watched with a quirk to her mouth as the man handed the sugary cereal to the child. She muttered, "Frustrated parents will do anything to survive."

While she'd been busy, the man and boy had started toward the front of the building. They moved alongside her. Her head jerked up to meet startling silver eyes.

Izzy cleared her throat. Had the man heard what she'd said?

He continued to watch her as if he knew she'd been focused on them. "Sorry we were so loud."

Izzy remained snared in his look, embarrassed that he might think she was judging him. "Not a problem."

Relief filled her as he moved on. She turned and watched him go. Tall, with a hint of gray at his temples, he looked as if he'd carried a burden on his shoulders for too long. Izzy shook her head. Tired from moving to a new town and learning a new job, she was ready to get home. Such as it was, being just a hotel room. Her own issues were enough without being concerned about a stranger and his problems. The current challenge consisted of cleaning up around her and paying for her groceries. She gathered her items into her arms again.

Making it to the checkout lanes, she went through the self-checkout while the man and the boy were in a line for a person at the cash register. A loud complaint came from behind her, and she didn't have to turn around to know it was the same little boy, Henry. "Candy."

She glanced over her shoulder to see the man patiently listening to the demand. If he were her child… Sadness swamped her. But he wasn't.

Izzy sent her items through the self-checkout and bagged them. The man and his child headed out to the parking lot. The noise level lowered by a half. She could have sworn a collective sigh came from everyone. It hadn't taken much to put the late afternoon Atlanta crowd on edge.

Finished with her business, she started toward her car. She'd chosen the first grocery store she'd come to on her way to and from Atlanta Children's Hospital from the efficiency hotel.

A giggle and an expletive drew her attention to the parking row one over from where her car sat. The man from earlier was picking up apples rolling across the asphalt. Henry sat in the buggy parked against the late model SUV.

The man really was struggling. Her heart went out to him. He needed help. Izzy hurried between the cars toward him, bending down to pick up apples.

He looked up from where he crouched, trying to pull an apple out from under a car tire. The man had the most beautiful eyes. They were like looking at quicksilver with a serving of intelligence in the depths. It was as if he could see more of her than she wanted him to. She blinked, registering the weary look on his face.

"Here you go." With a smile, she handed him a couple of apples.

He looked at her as he opened a bag with gratitude. She dropped the apples in. Henry squealed.

"I'll stand with him while you finish up here." She walked over to the boy. "Hi, Henry."

He settled and watched her with wide eyes.

"Do you have a dog?" Izzy asked.

The boy shook his head.

"How about a cat?" Izzy made sure to keep a hand on the cart so it wouldn't move.

Henry shook his head fast enough to make his eyes wobble.

Izzy couldn't help but grin.

The father joined them and put the bag of fruit in the vehicle. "Thanks for your help." He ruffled Henry's hair and took him out of the cart, giving him a hug. "Next time I'm going to make sure the bag is tied before I let you hold the apples."

Henry looked at the man with simple adoration.

A sweet sadness filled Izzy. There was obvious love between the two. She'd hoped to experience that with Richard and their child. Instead Richard had used her, thinking of only what he wanted. Izzy had no intention of ever getting caught in a one-way relationship ever again.

The man smiled, which was almost as striking as his eyes. "Thanks. You must think I'm a rubbish dad."

"You're welcome," Izzy said with a smile, "and no, I didn't. Anyone can have a bad day."

She started toward her car, glancing back at the man. She would likely never see him again.

Dr. Chad McCain pulled out his phone. He was needed in the ER. "I've got to go."

He left the hospital conference room without a backward look. After all, he'd gone to school to help children, not sit in meetings. He'd been on holiday for a week and was ready to return to work. He pushed through the double doors.

A nurse stepped beside him. "It's a boy with internal injuries from an automobile accident. He's in trauma one."

Chad didn't slow down. Yet everything in him wanted to turn around and go the other way. Instead he put his head down and forged forward. After Henry had been injured in the car accident that had killed Nan, his wife and Henry's mother, vehicle cases were hard for Chad to face. All he could see was his injured son, pale as death, laying on a too-large gurney.

His staff knew his history and always tried to warn him of what was coming. With a fortitude that came from who knows where, other than knowing a child needed him and that he had the skills to help, Chad strode into the trauma examination room. He prepared to go to work by pulling his stethoscope out of the pocket of his lab coat. The space was already filled with nurses and EMTs.

"We have a ten-year-old white male with a compound fracture to the left femur, a head laceration, problems breathing and possible internal injuries."

The voice came from the side and just behind him. It wasn't one he recognized as one of the usual nurses, yet it wasn't unfamiliar. He didn't have time to look and see who it was. With everyone having a mask on, he might not recognize her anyway. "Let me see what's going on here."

A space opened for him to move in next to the patient. With easy practice, he placed the ear tips of the stethoscope in his ears and the bell on the boy's chest. The patient's heartbeat was fast. Chad glanced at the monitor. And missing beats. He positioned the bell on the boy's side. His breathes were shallow. Chad moved the stethoscope down to the boy's mid-section. The gurgling sounds indicated internal injuries.

"Call the OR. This child needs abdominal surgery ASAP. The Ortho will have to wait. Let's get a set of X-rays."

"They're on the way."

There was that voice again. He just couldn't place it. "I want a blood panel, antibiotics and fluid running. Vitals?"

One of the nurses called out the numbers.

Beep, beep, beep...

The high-pitched sound originated from the monitor. The noise shocked everyone around him into action.

"The patient isn't breathing," Chad stated. "Start CPR." He placed his hands on the child's chest as a nurse placed a mask with a breathing balloon attached over his month. She squeezed in a rhythm.

"BP thirty over ten," someone in the group called.

"Crash cart!" Chad snapped without missing a beat.

"Here," the nurse whose voice he didn't know announced.

"Paddles?" He turned. His look met those of the nurse holding them. *Her!* He tensed. The woman from the store who'd helped him with the apples. What was she doing in his department? He felt mortified that she should have seen him at his worst, dealing with one of Henry's tantrums.

The nurse's eyes widened over the top of her mask. She recognized him as well. Chad took the paddles without hesitation, prepared to shock the boy back to life. Hovering them over the child's bare chest, he called, "Clear."

Everyone took a step back before Chad placed a paddle beside the heart and the other on the boy's side. "One, two, three."

With a beep from the machine, the boy's body came off the bed. As quickly as he turned to give the paddles back to the "apple" nurse, another nurse closed in to check the patient's vitals.

Chad glanced at the monitor, apprehension making his muscles tight. "Let's go again." The "apple" nurse had the paddles ready when he turned to her. He followed the same procedure. This time the monitor issued a steady beat. With a heaving sigh, he gave the paddles back.

"Okay, people." Relief sounded in his words. "We have him back. Now let's keep him alive long enough to get him to surgery. Let the OR know we're on the way. Then notify Ortho they're going to need to take care of the leg."

"Already done," the voice that belonged to the "apple" nurse said.

Chad nodded. Whoever she was, the woman was an efficient nurse. One he'd be glad to work with any day. He just cringed at the thought of how she must see him.

He checked the monitor. The boy's blood pressure remained low. "He's still in trouble. Give him two liters of oxygen. Let's get that blood work drawn, X-rays done and fluids in so this boy can be off to surgery ASAP. We don't have time to waste here."

Chad again listened to the boy's chest. He pursed his lips. His breathing remained shallow. It would be his guess that he'd broken some ribs as well.

The "apple" nurse said, "They're ready for him in the OR."

Relief washed over him. He accepted death could be a part of his job, but he didn't like letting it win any more than he had to. Between almost losing his son and the death of Nan, he knew well how special each day was. It made him a better doctor and father. He was determined to keep death at bay as often as humanly possible.

He remained with the patient until the surgery nurses came to get him. With that done, Chad started out of the trauma room, with one thought in his mind: Who was this new nurse?

Izzy felt more than saw the doctor follow her to the circular unit desk. Never in a million years would she have guessed he'd show up in the ER. She'd been as surprised and mortified to see "grocery" doc as his eyes indicated he'd been to see her. This was the last place she'd expected to see him.

"Imagine my surprise when you turned up in my ER today." His deep graveled voice came from behind her.

Izzy turned to face him. "No more than mine."

His brow rose. "At least here you won't have to pick up my apples."

She grinned. "I hope not."

"Henry and I didn't make a very good first impression. I'm sorry about that."

His expression reminded her of a sheepish little boy's. "Not a problem."

He waited to speak for a moment. "You ever

have one of those days when things just don't go your way?"

Like the day she came home to find Richard in their bed with another woman. "More often than I'd like to admit."

"That day in the grocery was one of those days. Anyway, it's a small world. By the way, I'm Dr. Chad McCain. Lead ER doc."

"I'm Elizabeth Lane. New head staff nurse."

He gave her a wry grin. "You won't hold my grocery-buying skills against me, will you? I assure you, my medical skill are far superior."

She made a noise in her throat. "I'm glad to hear it."

Izzy watched him walk away toward an exam room. Taking a seat behind the curved unit desk, she logged into the computer and pulled up a chart. A tech and a nurse sat not far away.

"I see you finally met our Dr. McCain. He was in rare form this morning," the tech said.

"I guess he was." Izzy wouldn't make any comment that might get back to the doctor.

"Yep." The nurse clicked a key. "He's great, isn't he?"

Another nurse shrugged. "He's one of our favorites around here."

"It must be hard on him, handling these

types of cases." The clerk passed the nurse a piece of paper.

"I'm sure seeing a boy injured in a car wreck reminds him of almost losing his own son in one. But he remains professional no matter what the case looks like. He holds it together somehow."

Izzy wouldn't ask what they meant. What had or hadn't happened with Dr. McCain wasn't her business. She wouldn't want anybody to share her history as gossip. Thankfully she could keep her gullibility where Richard had been concerned to herself. She'd made a change to a new town, a new hospital and a new job. She wanted a clean start. Not to see the look of pity on everyone's faces because they knew what Richard had done to her.

One patient after another kept the ER busy right through the afternoon. It wasn't until then that the patient care slowed enough for her to go to her shoebox-sized office down a short hall off the main part of the department. She had a meeting the next morning to prepare for.

As head staff nurse, she'd spent most of her time the past week reviewing how the department operated. Part of her job was to see that the Emergency Department ran smoothly and the doctors had what they needed when they needed it.

As a pediatric nurse, her duties also included assisting during acute injuries or when a member of the nursing staff was out, otherwise she handled the scheduling of nurses and reporting of data to the administration. She liked the patient-care aspect far more than the paper pushing.

Two days later, while Izzy was deep into material she had been busy building into a presentation one evening, there was a sharp knock at her office door. Her head popped up in surprise.

Dr. McCain stood in her doorway. He cocked his head toward the main part of the department. "I need your help. We have a burn patient coming in. I want someone with me who has experience."

Izzy pushed back her chair and followed him out the door. "How do you know I have burn experience?"

"Checked up on you."

"Do you check up on all the new nurses?" She wasn't sure how she felt about that.

"No, but I made an exception with you."

He must have read on her vita she had worked six months in a burn unit. Apparently she measured up. She hadn't felt lately as if she did. At least not in her personal life. "What do we have coming in?"

"A six-year-old with a full-thickness burn to his back, arm and hand." His words were tight, surrounded by anger.

"Do I want to know how it happened?"

He glanced at her, his mouth in a straight line. "No, you don't."

Izzy winced. She hated these cases. They stayed with her too long.

As they passed the unit desk, the tech said, "ETA three minutes," and handed them each a mask. Controlling infection with a burn was paramount.

Dr. McCain's stride lengthened, and Izzy hurried to keep pace. They reached the large automatic glass doors to the sound of the ambulance siren. It abruptly went off, indicating the ambulance was turning into the hospital. Once it was backing up to the door, Izzy and Dr. McCain hurried out to meet it.

She could smell burnt skin before she saw the boy. The EMT lifted the gurney out of the ambulance. The boy lay on his stomach with his face turned to the side. He was pale as the sheet that lay over him. It was held up by a towel rolled at his side so his skin wasn't touched.

Dr. McCain already had his stethoscope off and on the uninjured side of the boy's chest as they walked inside the unit.

"Trauma room three," Izzy told the EMTs.

An EMT started his report. "Six-year-old white male. Unresponsive. He has morphine on board to manage the pain. He passed out halfway here. The cause of the burn was boiling water down the right back, right arm and hand. Full-thickness burns. Injury happened forty-five minutes ago. Respirations are slow and heart rate low but steady."

Izzy swallowed hard. Nothing about the report sounded positive except it wasn't a grease burn, where the cleaning became more difficult. Still the boy would carry the scars from this day forever.

"This area needs to be a sterile as possible." Dr. McCain stopped outside the room and quickly pulled on a paper gown and plastic gloves. Izzy followed suit.

In the room Izzy hooked the boy up to monitors. Other staff entered, gowned and gloved, going to work beside her and Dr. McCain. Each knew their assigned job. Izzy relinquished the monitor setup to the other nurses and techs. Instead she turned to help Dr. McCain remove the ice packs placed on the burnt areas, then picked up the sheet covering the skin and handed it over to him, both of them careful not to touch the boy's skin.

Izzy winced at the red angry burn.

Dr. McCain didn't slow down his orders. "I need a CBC and full panel here. Also an electrolyte level. Temp?"

"Ninety-six," Izzy reported.

"Turn on the heater. People, it's going to get warm in here. Nurse Lane, let's put a catheter in, check fluid outflow. We also need a good central line in place with fluids and antibiotics running."

Over the next few minutes, she worked with Dr. McCain to get the catheter placed by rolling the boy toward her while Dr. McCain worked at his front. She placed the central line in the boy's unburnt arm. Another nurse saw to hanging and starting the fluids.

Despite all the movement of him and around him, the boy remained comatose.

Dr. McCain spoke to her. "It's time to get him bandaged and up to ICU. We'll leave the rolled towels where they are and let the saline run into them."

Izzy spoke to a tech. "We're going to need more towels in here. Lay them under the bed to catch the runoff."

A nurse pushed a cart with bottles of saline on it beside Izzy. She opened and handed Dr. McCain a bottle. He slowly pored the sterile water over the burn site. The blistered area made Izzy cringe. She lifted the boy's hand and arm with her palm, being careful not to touch any injured area.

Dr. McCain continued to go through bottles of saline, making sure the areas were all clean. In several places, he removed the dead skin, making sure the pink skin below showed. "Now for the silver sulfadiazine."

Izzy handed him a large scrub with a sponge on the end filled with medicine.

His eyes met hers over the mask as he nodded. When that one sponge had been used, he handed it to Izzy and she gave him another. Slowly and meticulously Dr. Cain applied the medicine. She couldn't help but be impressed. He worked efficiently, carefully and compassionately as he gently spread the ointment.

"You ready to start bandaging?" He looked at her.

"I am." She picked up a large roll of gauze and moved around beside him.

Dr. McCain wrapped the gauze while she saw to it that he had what he needed. A few times she held it in places as he positioned the next swathe.

"Talk to me, people. I need to know temp, heart rate, respirations, urine output. Someone needs to notify ICU we're sending them a patient. Also get Dr. Huff on the phone. I need to talk to him about this boy."

In an organized order, different staff members reported to Chad as he and she continued wrapping.

With bandages in place, Chad said, "Let's get this boy upstairs."

A couple of techs and a nurse pushed the patient out to the elevator.

"You did good work in there, Dr. McCain." Izzy gathered up supplies.

"Make it Chad. You weren't half bad yourself." He smiled.

Izzy's stomach dipped. The man had an extra nice smile. "You can call me Izzy."

"Izzy Lane." He looked off as if in serious thought. "It makes me think of the Beatles song 'Penny Lane.'" He hummed a few lines and grinned.

She quirked one side of her mouth. "Yeah, I've heard that before."

His face straightened and he looked at the clock. "Got to go. Henry's waiting. By the way, thanks again. Great job." He headed toward the exit, notes from the song "Penny Lane" following him.

They washed over her like a gentle breeze. She and Chad had apparently formed an unlikely team.

* * *

On Friday evening after work, Izzy stopped by a local restaurant for supper before she went home to her lonely hotel room. All she wanted tonight was to sit down to a meal and have a peaceful weekend. It had been an interesting couple of weeks.

Her first one had involved more paperwork and study of policy and procedure and meetings than actual administrating in the ER. The second week had been busy, exciting and challenging. Just learning people's names and personalities had been a full-time job. Most of the staff had been welcoming and helpful. Best of all, they showed her no pity.

She entered the local burger restaurant a nurse had recommended. Looking around, she winced. There wasn't an empty table in the room. So much for her meal out. Apparently fast food would be her only option this time of day.

A large hand waving in the air drew her attention. It was Chad with Henry sitting in a booth along the side wall. Her eyes widened when he waved her his way.

She approached the table. Going through a drive-through and eating in her hotel room alone had no appeal.

Chad asked as he stood, "Would you like to sit with us?"

She and Chad had tentatively found their way working with patients, but she wasn't quite sure they were ready for social situations. Izzy looked past him to Henry who had a fork and a knife in his hand and beat the ends on the table. This wasn't her plan for a restful evening, but how could she politely excuse herself?

"Thank you. That would be nice." Izzy slid into the booth.

Chad sat next to Henry, who was in a booster seat on his side of the booth. "Henry, sit down please. This is Ms. Lane. We met her at the grocery store. She works with me."

"Hi, Henry." Izzy settled on her seat. "Your wife won't mind me being here?"

"I'm a widower." Chad's tone came out flat with no sadness, but a note of being resigned to the status.

"Oh, I'm sorry I didn't know." How sad he had no one and Henry didn't have his mother. Still, relief washed through Izzy. She'd never do to another woman what had been done to her, and felt relieved she wasn't keeping him from a partner. Being faithful and loyal were important in a committed relationship. She took them seriously.

With a wide-eyed look, Henry watched her, then went back to waving the silverware around.

Chad caught Henry's arms. "Henry. It's time to settle down."

Henry did so but began to beat the utensils on the table again. Chad removed them from his hands and Henry yelled a protest.

Everyone in the restaurant stopped and turned toward them.

"Henry!" Chad hissed. "Shh." He placed his hand on the boy's shoulder.

Henry grabbed for the fork and knife, but Chad took them away, placing them out of his reach.

Henry squealed.

"Henry, would you like to draw me a picture?" Izzy picked up the coloring sheet and crayons that were on the table. She pushed the sheet toward Henry, then handed him one crayon.

The boy scribbled wildly.

Izzy placed her hand over his. "There's not another page so you need to make this one last."

Henry's eyes widened in surprise. She removed her hand. He went back to coloring but more like he should for his age.

Chad gave her an appreciative smile and relaxed in his seat. "You've done that more than once."

"Yeah, a few times. I have nieces and nephews. A little redirection almost always works." Izzy wished she could say she'd done the same with her own children.

"Kids take a lot of energy," Chad said.

"They do, especially after a long day at work." But she'd have liked to have that feeling of exhaustion.

A server came to their table. He handed Chad and her menus.

Izzy ordered her drink.

Henry's voice rose. Chad placed his hand on the boy's arm.

Chad was trying with his son. It must be difficult to discipline when he thought about almost losing his child in a wreck. Izzy leaned across the table. "You're being so good, Henry, that I'm going to give you another crayon."

Henry's attention remained on her as he took the crayon.

Chad shook his head and looked at her in wonder. "Miracle worker. Your children must be the best-behaved around."

Izzy cringed. A band tightened around her chest. She'd wanted children. Had even missed some of her best years waiting to have them. "I don't have any children."

"Well, you've missed your calling." Chad grinned, making him more handsome.

That band eased some. "I hope to have some one day."

Concern filled his eyes. "I didn't see anything about a Mr. Lane on your vita. Is there one somewhere?"

"No."

The waiter returned with her drink and asked to take their order. Chad ordered a hamburger plate for him and a child-size for Henry. She requested a large salad.

"You need to try the burgers," Chad suggested.

"I'm afraid I couldn't eat all of it." Her appetite hadn't been the same since she'd left Richard.

"I still recommend a burger. You can always take the leftovers home. I promise it's great."

Izzy looked at the server. "I'll have the burger plate then."

Chad grinned. "I don't think you'll be disappointed."

"I'm not as afraid of being disappointed as I am of not being able to get in my clothes tomorrow."

He studied her a moment. "From what I've seen, you don't have anything to worry about that."

Thought failed her. Was he flirting with her? She looked at Henry. He had stopped coloring. She covered her embarrassment by asking, "May I see your picture?"

Henry pushed the paper toward her.

"This is so pretty. You're doing such a good job." She returned the page to him. Henry went back to his coloring.

Chad looked at her in wonder. "You make it look so easy."

"It's not. I just happen to be lucky that it's working."

"I'm ashamed to say I was too busy building my career to be around as much as I should have been. You know what kind of hours we keep in the ER. I didn't spend as much time with him as his mother. If I had, maybe he'd be better for me."

Guilt at perhaps having judged him washed over Izzy. Now some of his actions with Henry made more sense.

"Even months later we're still learning to live together. We aren't doing a great job of it at the grocery store I'm afraid, but we're surviving."

"It can't be easy. It'll just take time. You have it. Henry is young. You'll both catch on. How long has it been since your wife died?"

"Nan's been gone thirteen months." He

mussed Henry's hair. "We're slowly learning to adjust. Most of Henry's behavior can be blamed on me. I indulge him. I realized after Nan was gone she'd done more than her share of parenting. Henry and I have had a major learning curve."

Izzy reached across the table and laid her hand over his for a moment. "I'm sure you've just been doing what you need to do to survive."

"Yeah, something like that." He didn't sound too sure.

The server returned with their meals.

Izzy's brows and voice rose. "Oh, my gosh, look at all this food." She glanced at Chad and found him grinning. "You actually thought I could eat all of this?"

He added ketchup to his plate. "Maybe you'll have to have a take-out container, but I think you'll like the burger." Chad cut Henry's sandwich into four pieces. He asked Henry, "Do you want ketchup to go with your fries?"

Henry nodded.

Chad looked directly at the boy. "I want you to be careful with the ketchup. If you're not, you can't have any more."

Henry eyes turned serious, and he nodded again.

With Henry settled, Chad's attention returned to her. "What brought you to Atlanta? I saw you had been living in Nashville."

Why she'd moved to Atlanta wasn't something she wished to discuss. She had to keep it simple and keep her secrets. "I just needed a change, and the staff nurse job was open. I've been wanting to move up."

"I bet they weren't happy when you left." Chad took a large bite of his burger.

"They weren't." She gave him a weak smile. "It's always nice to be wanted."

Chad could tell Izzy's smile didn't reach her eyes. He knew well what it was to have someone look at him like that. Before the accident that took her from him, Nan had done the same. She had been as saddened by the slowly deteriorating relationship as he. For years she'd felt neglected. He was sorry for that. It hadn't been his intention.

She'd understood the idea of a doctor keeping long hours but hadn't liked the reality. He hadn't either but that was part of the profession. She'd covered her anxiety well until the last few years of her life. They had talked about a divorce at one point but soon learned she was pregnant.

Chad believed children should have both their mother and father together. By that time, he'd seen too many fights between divorced parents when emotions were running high over an injured child. He'd wanted better for Henry. Had wanted the marriage to work. He'd tried harder at the end, but it was too little too late. He hadn't succeeded. It wasn't long before Nan died that he'd learned she was having an affair. Anger and guilt fought to overtake each other, which soon turned to bitterness.

Henry could be a handful. The problem was Chad couldn't bring himself to be tougher on him. He and Nan might have had their issues, but he loved Henry dearly. He'd almost lost Henry in the accident.

Izzy praising Henry brought Chad out of his gloomy thoughts. "You've been doing such a good job. What a big boy you are."

She was great with Henry. He responded to her. She encouraged him to behave and gave him affirmation for doing so. Izzy worked magic as far as he was concerned. "Had you always lived in Nashville?"

Izzy's gaze met his. Intelligence swam in her eyes along with a flicker of weariness and pain. What had happened to put that there?

"I'm Nashville born and raised."

"That must have made it hard to leave." He watched her.

"Yes and no."

"That sounds like a story." One he really wanted to hear for some reason.

"It was just time."

She wasn't going to give him the reason why, and he wouldn't ask directly. It wasn't his business. "I guess you worked at Vanderbilt University Hospital?"

"Actually, I was at St. Vincent out on the west side."

He popped a fry in his mouth. "I know that hospital. It's a good one."

She brightened with pride. "I like to think so."

Izzy wasn't freely giving information. "Then the opportunity opened down here, and you decided to take it?"

"Yes." Izzy sounded as if she was finished with this line of questioning. "It was a good opportunity to make a positive step in my career. This burger really is good by the way."

Her embarrassed look made him smile.

She opened her mouth wide to take a bite. "I'm glad you insisted on me getting it. I can't believe I ate almost all of it."

"I knew you wouldn't be disappointed." He picked up the bill the server left.

When Izzy reached for her purse, Chad said, "I'll get this."

"I don't want you to do that. I barged in on

you and Henry. I'm the one who should be paying."

"We were happy to have the company. Weren't we, buddy?" Chad looked at Henry, who had returned to coloring.

Izzy scooted out of the booth. "I'll agree if you promise that next time you'll let me pay."

"Okay." Would there be a next time? Chad hoped there would be. He'd enjoyed his time with Izzy, found her interesting. "Consider it my thanks for helping make me and all the others around us have a peaceful meal."

Izzy chuckled. "You're welcome but I don't think I did anything miraculous."

"It depends on who you ask." He left money on the table, took Henry's hand and their group made their way to the door. He placed his hand at her back to guide her toward it. Izzy stiffened and glanced over her shoulder. Seconds later she relaxed as they stepped through the crowd waiting for seats.

Outside on the sidewalk, Izzy turned to him. "Thank you for the meal." She looked down at Henry. "I enjoyed being with you."

Chad liked the way she included Henry in her thanks.

Henry wrapped his arms around one of Izzy's legs. "I like you."

Izzy went down on a knee and hugged Henry. "I like you too."

For some reason Chad felt jealous of his son. Chad could use a hug as well. He wasn't going to let that happen. "Can we walk you to your car?"

"I'm just over there." She pointed a few cars down. "Have a nice weekend, guys." Izzy waved a hand over her shoulder.

Chad watched Izzy until she was safely in her car. For them having had a slightly awkward start, he had learned to appreciate Izzy's skills in the ER, and now as a friend.

CHAPTER TWO

A WEEK LATER while Izzy sat at the unit desk, one of the nurses asked, "Have you found an apartment yet?"

"I've been looking but I can't find anything that I can afford or is what I want."

Another nurse asked, "Have you tried Garden Greens?"

Izzy nodded. "I called them yesterday. There's nothing until after the university semester ends. Staying in a hotel room is getting old and expensive. I'd really like to find an apartment above someone's garage. Somewhere I could have a little something that's really my own."

"Maybe you could look in Virginia Highlands," the first nurse offered. "Those are older homes with nice yards. A family-type area. A number of them have garages with a room above."

The unit tech swiveled in her chair to face

Izzy. "Have you been looking through the ads? Or going online?"

Izzy pushed at her hair. "I've done it all. I just can't seem to find what I want."

The tech picked up the ringing phone. Her face turned serious. "Near-drowning on the way in."

Everyone sobered. Izzy groaned. Those cases were some of the worst. They were never good. The recovery, if there was one, was long and discouraging. They almost always resulted in brain damage.

"I heard," Chad said from right behind them. "Which exam room?"

She watched Chad head toward the double doors to the ambulance bay with the nursing team assigned to him for the day following.

He had made the last week interesting. Any time he passed her in the unit or went by her office door, she heard the tune "Penny Lane." Her immediate impression had been of someone serious, but it turned out he had a sense of humor. Mostly at her expense. More amazing was she didn't mind. It had been a long time since someone had noticed her enough to tease. She'd lived with a man for years who never bothered to tease her or give her a sweet nickname. She and Chad didn't know each other well but he still had her smiling. It was a salve to her battered self-esteem.

Later that afternoon Izzy still had her head buried in paperwork and forms she'd been working on most of the day. A knock at her office door made her look up to see Chad leaning against the door, looking unsure.

"Hey. Am I needed?"

Chad waved her back into her seat.

He moved over to the single metal chair in front of her desk and slumped into it. His knees knocked against her desk, and he sat straighter.

"I have something like one of those rooms above the garage that I heard you were talking about. Except mine is behind the garage."

She wasn't sure how to react to that statement. Was he offering it to her? "You do?"

"I do. It needs some work. I'd have to move a few things around but if you'd like to look at it, you're welcome to."

"Are you offering to let me rent it?"

His eyes met hers. "Yes, isn't that what I said?"

It hadn't been but she had no intention of debating that. "I suppose it was. If you've been using it, then why would you let me move in?"

"Because you need a place to stay, and I have one."

Did she want to live so close to someone she

worked with? Or was it living so close to him? What would the others in the department think if she lived in his backyard? "I don't know."

He rose. "Come look or don't. I just thought I'd offer. You can always be looking for another place. It's better than a hotel room. That I can promise."

Uncertainty filled her but Chad did make the place sound appealing. She needed a home and he had one. What could go wrong? "I can't promise anything, but I'll come check it out."

"I know what you're thinking."

She couldn't imagine he did.

"That you'll have to put up with the noise of a kid. I promise you won't. Ms. Weber will see that he stays out of your hair when I'm not there. I promise we'll respect your privacy."

"That wasn't at all what I was thinking." She grinned, giving him a teasing look. "A little sensitive about Henry's noise level? I like Henry. Who's Ms. Weber?"

"She's an older neighbor who acts as my nanny. And maybe I'm the one who's a little sensitive about Henry." A contrite expression came over his face, giving him a boyish air. He looked away.

"You shouldn't be. He's a nice kid. If you haven't noticed, I work in a children's hospital so therefore I like children. Henry wouldn't be my reason for not taking the apartment, I assure you."

"Just come see the apartment. Then you can decide. Deal?" He put out his hand.

She looked at it for a moment before slipping hers into it. His larger one enveloped hers. Electricity shot through her all the way to her toes. She mumbled, "Deal," and pulled her hand away.

What was that reaction to Chad? A man she'd only known for a few weeks. One she worked with. It was unnerving at the least. There was no space in her life for those types of feelings. They couldn't be trusted.

On Saturday afternoon Chad watched Izzy pull into his drive. He'd trimmed the grass between the double cement lanes that morning. She parked behind his SUV sitting in front of the garage.

"Come on, Henry. Ms. Izzy is here." Chad smiled as Henry dropped the truck he'd been playing with and started toward the back door.

Izzy climbed out of her car. She drove one of those mini cars his legs wouldn't fit in. Yet it suited her petite body. When had he started noticing her height? Wearing a simple green T-shirt, jeans and sport shoes, she looked more like a college student than the woman in charge at the hospital. Izzy had seamlessly blended in with the staff and quickly become invaluable to the department. And him. He found himself wanting her at his side during the most difficult cases.

Chad went down his back steps. Reaching the yard, he turned to find Henry pushing the screen door as far as he could before he let it go. Chad winced when it slammed shut. "Henry, I've asked you a thousand times not to slam the door."

The boy ran past him straight to Izzy and wrapped his arms around her leg.

Chad hurried after him, fearing Henry might knock Izzy down.

She rocked on her heels and gave him a hug. "Hi, Henry."

Chad grabbed her elbow, steadying her. A shot of awareness went through him before he let her go. Izzy's gaze met his as she patted Henry's back.

"Play with me?" Henry asked, looking at Izzy with adoration.

"I can't right now. Maybe later. You dad needs to show me something. I'm going to see if I'd like to live here."

Henry looked at Chad with an expression that reminded him of Nan. Pain, quickly followed by anger of what had been and what was not shot through Chad.

"Ms. Izzy live with us?"

A stricken expression came over Izzy's face as she let go of Henry.

Chad hurried to correct his son. He placed a hand on Henry's shoulder. "No, she'll live in the apartment. Let's show it to her?"

Henry straightened his shoulders and took Izzy's hand. He marched along the stone path around the back of the garage.

Chad followed. "I don't think I got to say hello. I'll try to control Henry's exuberance in the future."

She smiled. "Hi. It's nice to have someone glad to see me."

Chad had been looking forward to Izzy's visit as well for some reason. He just hadn't shown it as clearly as Henry. The question was why? He enjoyed being around her. Teasing her. He'd dated some since Nan but none of the women had captured his attention as Izzy did. She was attractive, but others were equally so—there was just something about Izzy that appealed to him. Not that he would act on it. That wouldn't be fair to her. He would never make promises again.

Henry let go of Izzy's hand. He waited on

her to open the door before he stomped into the room. Soon she and Chad joined him.

Chad looked around the area, seeing it as she must. It was large with a partition built in one corner that created privacy for the bathroom. The kitchenette was stationed in the front corner. The rest was open space with a bed on one wall and an old leather couch and chair facing a large picture window that looked out to the backyard. The place looked neglected and worn.

He cringed. It really wasn't inviting. He'd be shocked if Izzy agreed to stay. "I'm afraid it's nothing fancy. If you do want to rent, you're welcome to do anything you wish with it. I haven't been back here in a long time. I'd forgotten how rough it looked."

She laughed. "You really shouldn't go into selling real estate."

He quirked one corner of his mouth. "You'd be welcome to share the yard. First come, first serve on the garage. I can also promise you privacy. Am I doing better?"

"Those are selling points." Izzy grinned and stepped over to the kitchen area. She stood beside the L-shaped counter with the sink on one side, the stove on the other.

He joined her but stayed on his side of the counter. "I'm afraid there's not a dishwasher."

"That's not a problem. There're only a few dishes when there's just one person."

"If you want to do any gourmet cooking, you're welcome to use my kitchen." He loved to share a homemade meal. It had been too long since he'd eaten something he hadn't heated up in a microwave.

"What you have here should be fine for anything I cook." She wandered over to the other corner and peeked into the bathroom.

"I know the couch and chair aren't much. Of course, you're welcome to bring any of your own furniture. I can get rid of this—" he touched the top of the sofa "—if you'd rather have something else." Nan had hated his college furniture so much she'd banished it to the apartment as soon as she could. He'd always liked the set.

Izzy continued to walk around the room. "I love leather furniture. The chair looks perfect to curl up in." She went to stand in front of the picture window. "This view is wonderful. The big oak tree is perfect. It's like living in a treehouse. Swiss Family Robinson's house at Disney World has always been my favorite."

"That's what you'll think until the nuts start falling. And the sun streaming in wakes you in the morning."

"I'll just put up some blinds or curtains."

She looked at him with a crease lining her forehead. "If that's okay with you?"

"Sure. Do anything you want to with the place." Noticing a dirty spot on the wall, he said, "I should have given it a coat of paint before I offered it to you."

"I can do that. Is egg-white okay with you?" She studied the space.

"I don't want you have to do that." The woman was a dynamo in a small package.

"I don't mind. I like fixing places up." Her eyes shined brightly as if she were already making plans.

He opened his hands palms up. "Then help yourself."

She continued to circle the space. "There are even shelves for books. This is much nicer than a hotel room. Thank you for offering it to me. I'll take it."

Chad was aware he had no business being so excited about her agreement to live there. What was he doing? He was going to be her landlord and she was going to be his tenant. They were colleagues. That was it. Still, she was a breath of fresh air in his stale world.

Her sad eyes got to him. He wanted to know what she was thinking when she looked at Henry the way she did. There was just something about Izzy that made him want to get to know her better. Discover the secrets he suspected she hid behind those large dark eyes. He couldn't—wouldn't—let his thoughts or actions go beyond friendship. "Henry and I promise not to intrude on you."

She waved that idea away. "How much is the rent?"

He told her a figure. Her eyes narrowed. "That sounds like too little, but I'll take it."

"Good."

"When's a good time for me to move in?"

He grinned as he stopped Henry from jumping on the sofa. "Whenever you're ready."

"Then I'll go to the hotel and get my belongings now. I'll be back in an hour or so. Is the water running and electricity on?" She'd morphed into the business mode he recognized from working with her at the hospital.

"The water is, and by the time you get back, I'll have flipped the switch for the electricity."

She started toward the door. "Good. I'd prefer not to start my time here living by candlelight."

Chad could only imagine how lovely she would look by candlelight. An image he shouldn't be picturing. These thoughts couldn't continue. Why were they there anyway? After Nan, he'd closed his heart off. He wouldn't allow a woman to crush him like she had done.

Life was too short to live in misery. After all, he'd learned pretty harshly that he wasn't good at relationships.

"Come on, Henry," he called. The boy had found one of his old toys near the sofa. "We've got a new tenant and we should go and let her be." Chad picked up his son.

"Izzy?" Henry's arms went out to her.

Chad chuckled and ruffled his hair. "No, you don't. You're going with me."

"I tell you what, Henry. Maybe we can play one day this week. Okay?" Izzy offered.

The boy nodded.

She took his hand. "Then we have a date."

"We're going," Chad said to Izzy. "Do whatever you want with the place. Holler if you have any questions." He headed out the door. Why did he have a feeling his life might have just taken a right turn?

Izzy rolled into Chad's drive for the second time that day. She'd fallen in love with the area, his home and the apartment on sight. The neighborhood was exactly what she had been looking for. Completely different from the chrome and cement she'd lived in for so long. The simple, beautiful setting made her feel like she'd found home. The big oak tree sealed the deal.

Chad's house had charmed her as well. It had a porch across the front with columns that were larger at the bottom than they were at the top. Ceiling fans hung on each side of the porch with groups of chairs. Painted a light butter yellow, the house looked like a true 1920s bungalow.

A small bike with training wheels lay on its side on the rock sidewalk and a ball sat in the grass.

There was no doubt a child lived here.

Moving into Chad's backyard might not be the best emotional decision she could make, but she did love the setting. She would be living close to the hospital, in a neighborhood instead of a cold apartment building five stories up. It was the change she was looking for. In fact his house was everything she had ever wanted.

Izzy parked behind Chad's SUV. She'd hardly stopped the car when Chad was at her door.

"What can I help you carry?"

"Me too," Henry eagerly said.

She had retrieved her clothes from the hotel, then stopped at the local home supply store. There she'd bought cleaning supplies and other needs she'd made a note of. "Yeah. Anything you see in the car goes in. Thanks for the help."

"I should have gone with you to the hotel. I didn't think about it until you left. As soon as we get you unloaded, I need to put your number in my phone."

Something about being in Chad's phone seemed too personal. Yet necessary.

"You stopped to do a little shopping, I see." His voice held a note of humor.

The easiness of being comfortable enough with each other felt right. Richard had been so serious all the time. Why hadn't she seen that? Why hadn't she seen a lot of things? "Yes. I got that paint we talked about."

"I'll pay you for that," Chad insisted.

"That's not necessary."

He opened the passenger side door. "We'll argue about that later." Chad looked at the darkening sky. "We should get your stuff in before it rains." He picked up the two gallons of paint.

She gathered an armload of clothes.

"What about me?" Henry demanded.

Izzy handed him a bag.

"What else did you get?" Chad looked inside the car.

"Some towel racks for the bathroom. General cleaning supplies. When I moved, I didn't bring much with me. I have a few things in storage at my parents'. I'll go get them my next full weekend off."

"Where do they live?"

"They're still in Nashville."

Chad put down a can and pushed open the door of the apartment.

Izzy draped her load over the top of the couch. "Just put the stuff in the middle of the floor. I'll sort it all later."

They continued to make trips to the car until everything laid around her new home.

"Henry and I'll leave you alone to get settled. We'll be in the house if you need us." Chad hesitated at the door.

Did he want her to ask him to stay? "Thanks for your help."

"No problem. Come on, Henry." Chad reached out a hand. "We need to hurry if we don't want to get wet."

"I stay here," the boy wailed.

"Henry," Izzy said softly. "You can come visit tomorrow."

The boy quieted, his eyes wide.

"I promise." Henry needed a woman's attention. Izzy's heart went out to him. He missed his mother.

"See ya later." Chad and Henry left.

Why did she suddenly feel lonelier than ever?

* * *

Chad saw the flash of headlights from the kitchen window as Izzy pulled into the drive later that evening. He figured she'd gone for food. More than once he'd talked himself out of asking her if she'd like to come to his house to eat. Even Henry asked about Izzy.

A buzz filled the air having someone nearby. Or was it because it was Izzy? More than once he'd wondered how her settling in was going, but he stopped himself from disturbing her. He'd put Henry to bed and was taking out the trash when Chad saw her.

She stood in the yard with her arms in the damp air twisting one way and then the other stretching.

He walked toward her. "Hey."

Izzy jumped. "I didn't hear you out here."

"I promise I wasn't skulking around. I brought the trash out." He pointed around the corner of the garage. "How's it going?"

She brushed a lock of hair away with the back of her hand. "Pretty good. I'm probably going to be sore in the morning, but I've gotten some things done. I even managed to paint one wall."

"I should've been helping you with that." He would've if he hadn't had Henry to see to, or if she had acted as if she wanted his help.

"I didn't mind. It was the easy one. I'll do a little more over the next couple of weeks. It'll get done. Would you like to see?"

"Sure." Chad wasn't sure he should be entering her domain. Yet he was a landlord. He needed to check out the apartment every so often.

Inside, Izzy spread her arms wide. "A clean kitchen and a painted wall."

The wall behind the bed did look crisper and the kitchen gleamed. "You have been busy."

Chad stepped up to the chair and picked up one of a couple of packages containing bathroom towel rods. "You shouldn't have to do all these. I should have put them up before I told you about the place."

"I'll take care of installing them tomorrow."

"I'll can take care of them right now. Then maybe I won't feel so guilty about letting you do all the work in here." He skimmed the instructions.

Izzy sagged as a look of relief formed on her face. "Would you mind? Putting those up is really not in my skill set. I never get them tight enough."

"Here I was thinking you didn't have a deficiency in your skill set. I thought you could do anything."

She chuckled. "Boy, do I have you fooled."

Izzy did seem pretty perfect. "Let me get my tools and check on Henry. He should be asleep." Chad put the towel bars back where he'd found them.

Returning with his toolbox and a baby monitor, Chad picked up the holders and headed for the bath. "Izzy, come show me where you think these should go."

She came to stand in the doorway of the tiny room. "One needs to go on that wall and the other near the sink."

"I'm not going to put them up unless you show me exactly where you want them. Otherwise, I won't get them right." He tore open a package and handed a rod to her. "Show me."

He backed up so she could squeeze in front of him. Her back brushed his chest. Heat shot through him. It had been too long since he'd had a woman. Especially one that appealed to him as much as Izzy. She smelled of something sweet and healthy. Her hair felt like silk beneath his chin. What would she do if he kissed that bare spot between her hairline and the edge of her T-shirt? That was not something he would let happen.

She placed the holder on the wall. "Do you have something to mark this with?"

"Uh?"

"Pencil. Pen. Caulk?" She glanced over her shoulder.

Chad shook his head. "Yeah. Right here." He twisted and pulled a carpenter's pencil out of his toolbox. Reaching around her, his forearm brushed her breast as he marked the spot.

He felt more than saw Izzy tremble. "You get in the shower."

"What?" His body caught fire at the possibilities. Those thoughts had to stop.

"That way I have enough room to turn around to mark the other holder. Hand me that one."

He picked up the shorter bar and gave it to her.

Izzy took it and the pencil from him. She held it to the wall. After marking the spot, she said, "There, you should be all set. I'll leave you to it."

Chad watched the enticing swing of her hips as she walked out of the bathroom. How silly would he look fully dressed and soaking wet from a cold shower? He'd made a friendly offer to rent this place and now he was having these lusty ideas about his tenant. He must do better.

Forty-five minutes later he stepped out of the small space in firm control of his emotions. "All done."

"Great," Izzy said from where she made the bed.

Izzy and a bed Chad refused to think about. "I've got them as snug as I can. You shouldn't have any problem with them falling."

"I'm impressed. Good in an emergency and good with your hands." She fluffed a pillow and propped it against another on the bed.

Was Izzy flirting with him or just unaware of the innuendos she kept making? "You've no idea."

She looked at him with wide eyes and a quizzical expression, then blinked before her face turned beet red. "I...uh, didn't mean it the way it sounded."

Chad grinned. "I know what you meant. Thank you for the compliment. I'll reimburse you for the holders. I'll take it off your first month's rent."

"Thanks. If you keep this up, I won't have to pay any rent."

He stepped toward the door. Izzy joined him. Without thinking, he reached out and touched her cheek. "You've got a spot of paint right here."

Her gaze met his, held. "I imagine I have it all over me. A good shower should get rid of it."

She rubbed at the spot, her fingers touching his. Chad didn't even want to think about her taking a shower. The more he was around Izzy, the more all sorts of "wrong ideas" kept coming to mind. He wasn't looking for a serious relationship, which was something he suspected Izzy was after. So why was he so interested in her?

It had been a while since Nan's death, but the melancholy nature of their relationship hadn't faded. Or his part in the failure of the marriage. That wasn't a place he felt capable of going again. Lessons learned. Izzy didn't strike him as a woman who would be satisfied with anything less than commitment. Something he couldn't take a chance on giving again. Or carrying the guilt for. What if the marriage failed again? He wouldn't do that to Henry. Or himself. "See you later then."

"Thanks for offering me this place. This is so much better than a hotel room."

He needed to get back to the house. See about Henry. Think less about Izzy. "You're welcome. Have a good night."

Chad left before he was tempted to do anything more. Such as kiss her.

CHAPTER THREE

AT THE HOSPITAL five days later, Izzy was sitting behind her desk when one of the unit nurses came to stand at the door. "Izzy."

She glanced up. "Yes."

"We need your help. We're swamped with the two nurses out."

Izzy looked at the pile of papers on her desk. She'd just have to stay late and catch up. "Yeah. Where do I need to go?"

"Dr. McCain has a patient in exam room one. Suspected meningitis." The nurse hurried off.

After tugging her scrub top into order and pulling her hair back into a band, Izzy headed out the door. She arrived at the exam room as Chad walked up. He didn't pause, his face wearing a no-nonsense expression. After only a few weeks, Izzy recognized he was in doctor mode. He liked to tease but when it came to his patients, he turned serious.

They hadn't seen much of each other even in the last few days despite her living in his backyard. They weren't on the same schedule. A couple of times they had waved at each other as one of them came or went. Once she'd been pulling in as he backed out of the drive. She waited to let him out before she turned in.

Now he looked at the electronic charting pad as he spoke to the parents. "Hello. I'm Dr. McCain. I'm the ER doctor. I need to ask you some questions."

Izzy went to work recording the comatose ten-year-old girl's vital signs.

"Can you tell me what's going on?" Chad voice had gone low.

The mother spoke up. "Jeanie was playing in the backyard with a friend. She was fine, then she came in the house and said she wasn't feeling good. The next thing I knew she was throwing up. I touched her and she was burning up. She seemed confused when I ask her where it hurt." The pain and fear rang clear in the woman's voice.

Chad moved to stand across the bed from Izzy. The girl lay with her eyes closed, showing no reaction. As he pulled his stethoscope from his pocket, he spoke to Izzy, "Let's get a CBC and total protein panel along with a procalcitonin draw."

"Right away," Izzy told him. She picked up the electronic pad he'd set at the end of the bed. She punched in the order. She then watched as Chad checked the girl's eyes, gently pressed along the child's neck. Chad's tenderness of touch always amazed her.

He looked at her and said quietly, "We'll need to do a spinal tap."

Izzy stepped out of the room and returned with the prepared kit. Chad sat on a stool in front of the parents, and the father held the mother's hand.

Chad spoke in a grave tone. "Your daughter's very sick. I believe she has meningitis. Which is an infection in the brain and spinal cord. I can't be sure if it's a viral infection or fungal until tests are done. The neurologist will decide on the course of treatment when all the tests are in. Jeanie will be going to ICU."

The mother sobbed.

Chad's shoulders stiffened but he continued talking. "Jeanie's in the right place and will get the best of care here. I'll be peforming a spinal tap to remove enough fluid for testing in a few minutes. I'm going to ask you to wait in the waiting room until someone comes to get you. They'll show you where to go."

"We understand." The father stood and helped the mother up.

Chad patted the woman on the shoulder. "We'll do everything we can to help your daughter."

The parents stepped to the bedside and kissed their child. With tears in their eyes, they reluctantly left the room.

Izzy couldn't help but admire Chad's understanding bedside manner. Making sure to call the child by her name. That meant a lot to the parents. He had a way with people. He'd certainly charmed her in a short time.

"Izzy, let's get this spinal tap done and the sample to the lab."

They put on gowns, masks and gloves. Another nurse joined them.

"Roll her to her side," Chad said.

Izzy and the other nurse went to the other side of the bed from Chad. The assisting nurse stood at the girl's feet while Izzy went to her head. They rolled the girl, giving Chad a clear view of her back. He prepared a sterile area along the girl's spine, pressing his finger to find the spot between the vertebrae.

"Needle," Chad requested, and Izzy handed it to him.

Chad inserted a thin needle into the spinal cord and suctioned out fluid.

"See this gets to the lab right away." He

packaged it in a sterile package and handed it to the nurse.

Izzy cleaned up the tap area and put a bandage over the entry wound before throwing away the leftover supplies.

Chad said, "I'll send techs in to take her up to ICU. I have more patients to see. Thanks for the help, Izzy." With that, he was gone.

Hours later Izzy was back behind her desk, inputting the next week's schedule, when there was a rap on her door.

Chad stood there. "You're here late."

She sighed. "Yeah. Doing some actual nursing put my paper-pushing behind today."

He gave her a wry smile. "That happens. I finally have a break. You look like you could use one too. Would you like to join me in our lustrous cafeteria for dinner?"

Izzy grinned at his formal invitation. Looking at the papers on her desk, she shouldn't take Chad up on his offer for more than one reason. Yet she was hungry and did need a break. She'd missed their banter during the week. Pushing back from the desk, she said, "Thanks for asking. I'd love to."

"How've you been?" Chad asked as they strolled down the long hallway toward the elevators. "Your new home working out?"

"Yeah, it is." She grinned and teased, "Questionable landlord but otherwise great. I've been busy here. I'm still learning the ropes." Izzy looked at his profile. It was a nice one. For years she paid little attention to other men since she was committed to Richard. Yet she could say without a doubt that Chad was an extremely handsome man.

She couldn't remember the last time a man had asked her to dinner. Even to a hospital cafeteria. Richard had always expected her to have dinner waiting on her days off. He'd often asked her to pick something up on her way home from work. She'd been raised in a world where the wife took care of the meals. It was her mom's way of showing love.

When she started helping fund Richard's schooling, she'd hesitated for a moment but he had convinced her she'd be doing it for them. For their future. "Wasn't that what love was all about?" he would say. But his love was one-sided; she hadn't seen it.

"It's hard to believe you live fifty paces from me and I haven't seen you all week except in the driveway." Chad matched his pace with hers, seeming not to expect her to keep up with his long stride. Another difference between Chad and Richard. She needed to stop comparing them. It wasn't like one was going to replace the other.

"Yeah, our schedules have been opposites this week."

"Have you met Ms. Weber yet?"

"No. I've seen her coming and going a couple of times." Izzy pulled the shirt of her scrub into place.

"Then I'll make sure you meet her when we're all there at the same time. She walks over from her house to see to Henry. He often goes to her house as well."

Izzy had been working during the day and at night painting her apartment. "That sounds like a nice setup for you and Henry."

"It's working for now. As he gets older, I'll have to make adjustments." They stopped at the elevator bank. Chad pushed the down button.

The elevator dinged and the doors opened. They stepped inside. Just before the doors closed a group joined them, pushing Izzy and Chad toward a corner. His large frame warmed her all the way down her back. Izzy's body hummed with awareness of Chad standing near. She didn't dare speak for fear her nervousness would show. Neither did she move a muscle as they went down one floor.

Izzy felt dainty next to Chad's bulk. She released the breath she'd held when the doors opened, and they moved out. They continued behind the others to the cafeteria.

"I've only been down here one other time." Izzy looked around the space with tables and large glass windows.

"Where do you normally eat?" Chad looked at her.

"I bring my meals and eat at my desk or in the break room if I'm asked." She turned toward the serving lines.

His brows rose. "Asked?"

"The staff deserves to have some time when they can be themselves without the boss around. And to vent without being heard."

"That's considerate of you." Chad's admiration showed in his eyes.

She shrugged. "I know how it is. I've been in their position before."

"Still, you don't have to be so nice. Henry has good taste in women."

"Thanks." But did he feel the same way about her as Henry did? Why should it matter if he did?

Chad gave his lips a resigned twisted. "I hate to admit it, but I eat here most days. I'm not much of a cook. This is easy and convenient. It gives me a chance to get out of the unit. Sometimes I just really need to get away."

"So this is where you bring all your dates?"

His head swivel around.

Izzy winced. "I'm sorry. That was just a figure of speech."

He placed his hand over his heart. "Ouch. That hurt."

"That wasn't my intention. I just got out of a bad relationship. I'm not interested in dating anyone."

His gaze met hers. Reassuring and demanding at the same time. "What can be simpler than supper in a hospital cafeteria as a nondate?"

Izzy had no doubt her face had turned beet red. "I'm sorry that wasn't very nice and very presumptuous."

"I think I need to hear more about this lifechanging event but first let's get our food."

Izzy went through one of the three serving lines to get her food. She didn't want to go into her past over a meal with Chad. Yet she'd opened the door. Her aim had been to make it clear there wouldn't be anything more than friendship between them. She had to learn to believe in herself again.

They met again at the cash register. Chad let her go ahead of him. She stepped to the cashier.

Chad told the woman checking them out, "I'll get both of these."

Izzy narrowed her eyes at him. "I told you—"

"I know what you said but I asked you to keep me company." He handed some bills to the woman who watched the interaction between them too closely.

As they walked toward an empty table for four, Izzy said over her shoulder, "I thought I made it clear this wasn't a date."

"Then next time you can pay. Will that make you happy?" Chad walked close behind her.

"That's what you said last time. I already owe you for one meal." She stopped at a table near a group of windows where she could see the outside.

"So now you're keeping score." Chad settled into a metal chair as if he were looking forward to the world's best meal.

Somehow he'd managed to make her sound petty. She sat in the chair across the table from him.

Chad took a large bite out of his grilled cheese sandwich. Finished chewing, he then drank his drink through a straw. "Now tell me what brought on your attitude about dating."

"It's no real attitude. It's just as I said. I've come out of a bad relationship, and I don't wish to step into another one."

"And you think eating dinner with me would

be going back into a bad relationship?" He looked serious but there was a teasing note to his tone.

Izzy huffed. "That's not what I meant."

"I know. Is that bad relationship why you decided to move to Atlanta?"

"Let's just say I needed a change." If she'd known this would be the line of conversation when he'd asked her to dinner, she might have said no.

"That sounds ominous."

She had to put a stop to his interrogation. Shame washed through her. Admitting she'd been used by Richard wasn't something she wanted to share with Chad. With anyone for that matter. "I really don't wanna talk about this."

"Okay. What would you like to talk about?" He continued to eat.

"How about you telling me what's your favorite place in town?"

He leaned back in his chair and studied her a moment. "You really are avoiding the subject. But I'll go along. There're a lot of things about Atlanta I like. I think there's something for everyone. Certainly, the sports are nice. There's the art and natural history museums. The Fox Theatre brings in plays. Of course, Henry's favorite place is the zoo. I don't get to do as many things as I would like. Henry and my work keep me pretty busy."

"Maybe you could change that."

"I don't know. We only have so much time in a day, a week…"

Izzy pushed a piece of lettuce away. She'd wasted too many of her days, she thought. "Yeah, but Henry will only be young for a short while."

Izzy wasn't sure where this conversation was headed but she did appreciate learning more about Atlanta. She couldn't resist trying to figure out why Chad, who had a nice home, a good job and a precious child, wasn't in a serious relationship. What was wrong with him that wasn't obvious?

"Since we seem to be touching on the personal, would you tell me in more detail what happened to your wife?"

"She was killed in an automobile accident." A sadness came to his eyes before he said, "Henry was with her."

"That must have been awful." Chad's actions made more sense now.

He put his sandwich on the plate and wiped his mouth. "Worst day of my life. I don't know what I would have done if I had lost them both."

"I know yours and Henry's worlds must

have been turned upside down." She placed her hand on his for a moment.

"It was, but we're figuring it out. Mostly Henry is." Chad grinned. "I just do what he tells me to."

Izzy laughed. Something she hadn't really done in months. She liked Chad. Henry as well. Too much.

Three days later Chad hurried out the back door toward Izzy's apartment. He knew she was there because her car sat in front of his in the drive.

"Izzy," he called through the screen door.

"Yes?" Her voice came from somewhere near the kitchen.

"I need your help."

She opened the door with a worried look on her face. "Is Henry all right?"

"Yeah. I'm needed at the hospital for a few hours. They're short a doctor. Just a half shift. This is Ms. Weber's day off. Would you mind watching Henry for a few hours?"

"It's no problem. Give me five minutes and I'll come to your house."

He grinned. "I'll make this up to you. I promise. I really appreciate it."

"Not a problem. I had promised Henry a

playdate and this will give me a chance to do that."

He'd promised himself he'd stop working so many hours before Nan died but he couldn't tell the hospital no when they needed him. Work also helped him cope with the changes in his life after Nan. Even now with just Henry, Chad was making the same mistake. Izzy was right about time. It would pass quickly. But what could he do when he was needed?

Chad returned home just before dark to sounds he'd not heard in a long time, if ever. The noise of a child playing happily in the yard. Female laughter flowed over him like the sweet sound of a brook. He walked around the apartment to the backyard, where he found Henry swinging as Izzy pushed him. His son smiled as Izzy returned it. Chad wished he were included in that glow of happiness.

Izzy seemed to create that. As hard as he worked to keep her at arm's length, there was a greater tug to get closer to her so he could bask in the warmth. She'd radiated hurt when she'd talked about her past relationship. His heart had gone out to her. For a moment he had a fleeting idea that he could show her what a relationship should be like. The thought was laughable. Based on his marriage, he knew nothing about making a woman happy. What made him think he could do that for Izzy? Or that she would be interested in him doing so.

"Higher," Henry squealed.

"Like this?" Izzy gave him a push.

Henry's giggles filled the air.

Chad hadn't seen Henry this happy in a long time. He missed his mom. Needed a mother figure in this life.

"Daddy," Henry called.

"Hey, buddy. It looks like you're having a good time."

"I go high."

The smile Izzy offered was like bright sunshine on a cold winter day. His chest tightened. When was the last time someone had been truly glad to see him? Nan had gotten to the point where she hadn't even made the effort.

Henry slowed to a steady swing.

"Have you been having fun?" Chad stepped in front of Henry but not close enough to get hit.

He nodded four times. "We make cookies."

"That does sound like fun." He looked at Izzy. "I hope you didn't ruin your dinner."

She smiled. "Eating cookies for dinner isn't that big of a deal every once in a while. Isn't that right, Henry?"

The boy smiled.

Izzy gaze remained on Chad. "How did it go at the hospital? Super busy?"

"Busy enough." He moved to lean up against the tree. "Sounds and looks like y'all been having more fun here though."

"Henry, I think it's time for you to play in the sandbox. I'm gonna talk to your dad for a few minutes." Izzy slowed the swing and lifted Henry out of the child swing.

"Push me," Henry whined.

Izzy bent to look at Henry at eye level. "What did we talk about earlier?"

"I not whine?"

She smiled and cupped his cheek. "That's right."

Henry went to the sandbox nearby.

"Let's sit down. I know you must be tired." Izzy walked over to the two retro metal chairs sitting under the oak tree.

"I don't recognize these." He fingered the top of one of the yellow chairs.

"I found them at a yard sale just down the road. I thought they'd look nice here. Give me a good place to read."

"I like them." He appreciated most things Izzy had a hand in.

Satisfaction filled her smile. She took a seat.

Chad sank into the other chair. He rested his head back and closed his eyes. The last of the day's sunshine warmed his face. A breeze rustled the leaves. A sweet smell of something floral tickled his nose. Izzy's scent. He could enjoy that smell forever. "I really appreciate you watching Henry. I'm sure you're tired too."

She yawned "It's a good tired, I have to admit. Anything exciting happen in the unit?"

"Mostly the usual stuff. Small injuries, strep throats and a couple of rashes. I only had one admit." He paused. "Oh, and one aggressive mother making a pass."

"Oh, wow, you did have a big evening."

He huffed. "That's a nice way of putting it."

Izzy voice held humor. "The trials of being a handsome doctor. Not your type?"

"Nope. You think I'm handsome?" He raised a brow and grinned.

She huffed. "Don't even pretend you don't know you are a catch."

"Nan thought so until she didn't. She thought being married to a doctor would be wonderful. It wasn't. She ran around on me in the hope of finding some happiness because I couldn't give it to her." He couldn't look at Izzy. Instead he watched Henry, who had left the sandbox to swing a stick.

Izzy sucked in a shocked breath. "That is awful."

A shadow of sadness filled his eyes. "My

marriage was already on the rocks when Nan died. I'd asked for a divorce a few days before the accident."

She reached across the space between them and took his hand. "Chad, I'm so sorry."

"I am too. Marriage is supposed to be forever. My parents have been married for forty-five years. My grandparents for sixty-five. I thought Nan and I would be the same."

Pushing with his foot, he made the chair rock. "Nan had been unhappy for years. My work hours can be hard to live with. In hindsight we shouldn't have married. She needed more attention than I had time to give. Between finishing school and starting my career, there wasn't much time left. For that, I'm really sorry. We talked of divorce but then she found out she was pregnant. We decided to try to make it work."

He sighed. "But then I found out she was cheating on me. I had already seen a lawyer about filing for divorce when the police came to the hospital to tell me about the accident. I hated the idea of getting a divorce for Henry's sake, but he also needed parents who were happy together. I've often wondered if Nan drove off the road on purpose. I wouldn't have put it past her, but I'd like to think she wouldn't have taken that chance with Henry. So you can see you're not the only one with a screwed up relationship in your history."

Izzy squeezed his hand. "You didn't deserve that. You didn't do anything wrong."

He raised a shoulder and let it drop. "Maybe not, but it does still make me wonder what I could've done or should've done to make our marriage better. If there was a difference I could've made. Or worse would I have been willing to make? Apparently, I'm just not cut out for marriage. But I am determined to be a good father despite the hours I work. Henry is my complete focus when I'm not at work. That leaves little time for dating or romance."

Izzy moved her hand to her lap. "We always have people in our lives we aren't enough for no matter how hard we try. I'm not much better. I gave nine years of my life and my money to a guy to come home and find him in bed with another woman. I have no interest in making that mistake again."

"At least you knew when to get out." He wished she were still holding his hand. Somehow it made the pain of this discussion easier.

"I did, but it was hard. To have devoted that much time to someone who I felt cared about me as much as I did him and to learn he had been using me was devastating." Izzy looked at Henry. "You at least got something wonderful out of a bad situation."

"I did, didn't I?" He smiled fondly at Henry.

Izzy's voice took on a soft note. "It's obvious that you love Henry dearly. All the love and care you've given matters. It's never too late for that to make a difference."

"I hope it does. He's had a hard young life. How did we get on this unpleasant subject?"

She gave him a thin-lipped smile. "Apparently, we both needed to talk. I'm glad you felt you could tell me."

Which wasn't like him. He was working hard to put what he could in the past. "I think that's because you're easy to talk to."

"I'll take that compliment." She stood.

It was time for him and Henry to go to the house. What had him speaking so plainly to Izzy? He'd kept his distance from women. There had been a few dates but never any real involvement outside of the physical. Why did Izzy have him confessing to her?

Chad got to his feet as well. "It was meant that way." He reached out a hand. "Henry, it's time to go in."

The boy came to him.

Chad took Izzy's hand, playing with her fingers as he looked in her eyes. "You do know it was his loss, don't you?"

Her eyes glistened. "That might be the nicest thing anyone has ever said to me." She gave him a quick kiss on the cheek. "Thank you."

CHAPTER FOUR

IZZY SAT UNDER the oak tree the next morning, enjoying the cool before the heat of the day set in. She had been rethinking her conversation with Chad. What he'd said swam in her head. He had endured too much. Her heart went out to him. The idea his wife had treated him the way she had was incomprehensible. He hadn't deserved what happened to him, yet he'd been reassuring her.

Then he'd said something nice, and she'd kissed him. Even though it was on the cheek, it made it personal. He'd looked as surprised as she'd felt. They were both mature adults so surely he would have seen the kiss for the impulsive action was. She did. So why could she still remember the briny taste of his skin.

She must protect herself from the growing feelings she had for Chad. The more she was around the McCain males, the more she liked them. Sharing the evening with Henry had been like being a mother. She'd enjoyed every minute. What she didn't need to do was get used to it. Her living situation was temporary. Right now she was vulnerable emotionally. A rebound relationship would be fatal. She didn't trust her judgment where men were concerned, and she couldn't afford to make a mistake again. Love had blinded her once. She wouldn't let history repeat itself.

A good friendship, with boundaries was what she needed. She'd maintain distance, not become involved except on a superficial level. People did that all the time. Why couldn't she? All she had to do was keep her guard up. Being around Chad and Henry had helped her to start breathing again. To put her life together. She would always be grateful for that.

"Do you have anything planned outside of sitting under this big oak tree this weekend?" Chad asked as he walked up behind her.

"I have to work tomorrow but other than that I plan to read a book. I'm not even doing any painting. Why?"

"The people in the neighborhood are having a block party this afternoon. Ms. Weber is insisting that Henry and I come. You're a member of the neighborhood now. How about going with us?"

"I don't know." She paused a moment. Why

shouldn't she go? "If I went, what would I need to bring?"

Chad took the other chair, leaning forward, putting his elbows on his knees. "I don't know. It's covered dish, whatever that is. Henry and I were planning to carry rolls."

She laughed. "I think we can do better than that."

"*We.* I like the sound of that. But heavier on the *you* where cooking is concerned."

Izzy stood with her hands on her hips and glared down at him "Then *we* need to go to the grocery store."

"Back to the scene of the crime. Couldn't you just go and leave Henry and me here?" He gave her a pleading look.

She shook her head. "No. I think it'd be a good trip for you both. Henry could use some practice in that department."

He groaned. "There's is no mercy with you, is there?"

She shook her head, giving him her sternest look.

"Okay, if you insist." Chad stood.

"I do."

His shoulders sagged. "I'll get Henry and meet you at the car."

Izzy smiled at Chad's disgusted look. "I'll see you in a few minutes."

He started away.

"Uh, Chad, about that kiss last night. I shouldn't have gotten so personal."

He came to stand close, his gaze holding hers. "Not a problem. We both were talking about some heavy stuff. I appreciate you listening to mine."

When he turned and walked away, Izzy let out her breath. Why had disappointment filled her? Had she wanted him to kiss her?

Twenty minutes later she road to the store in Chad's SUV with him driving and Henry in the middle seat.

"Izzy?"

"Huh?" She sat in the front seat with her hands clasped in her lap.

"Do you plan to ever look at me again?" Chad's voice held humor.

"I'm not *not* looking at you." Her focus went to his hands on the steering wheel. They were capable hands—she'd seen them help children, lift Henry and touch her.

"In the eyes."

She glanced at him.

Chad grinned. "You can't avoid me forever."

She glared at him. "I can try."

A full-bodied laugh filled the SUV. "I'd like to see you try."

A few minutes later, he pulled into the grocery store parking lot. Henry squealed as she helped him out of the car seat. She bent to Henry's level. "You can't scream in the grocery store. You're going to be a good boy. If you're not, you'll have to come back out here and sit in the car. Do you understand?"

The boy nodded, his look fixed on her.

"Good. Then inside we go."

Chad pushed the cart with Henry in the seat as Izzy walked along beside them. She patted Henry's arm. "Remember, quiet voice."

Chad stopped the cart, looking back and forth as if deciding which aisle he needed to go down. "What're we going to fix?"

"I thought we'd make my mom's macaroni and cheese. How does that sound to you, Henry?" She leaned in close to him.

The boy smiled. "Mac and cheese."

She returned it. "I think Henry agrees. How about you, Chad?"

"Sound good to me."

She liked this too much. It felt as if they were a family. The pleasure of that idea was becoming fixed in her head. Couldn't she just enjoy it for a little while? It would only be temporary.

They continued around the store, gathering the supplies needed. At one point Henry became louder than necessary. She raised a brow in Chad's direction and he placed his hand on Henry's arm. "Don't be so loud."

The boy quieted down. Chad gave her a self-satisfied smirk as if he'd accomplished a life-saving procedure. She nodded her encouragement.

They kept moving around the store. It wasn't until they were in the checkout line that Henry started acting up again. His demands for candy rose to a yell. When Chad told Henry he couldn't have any, the scene escalated.

Izzy spoke to Henry, but it did no good. To Chad she said, "Why don't you take Henry to the car? I'll finish checking out."

Chad opened his mouth to argue.

Before he could say anything, she said, "I don't mind." Henry needed to learn a lesson. An immediate one given by Chad. She wouldn't always be around. That idea had her pausing for a moment, made her sad.

With Henry kicking and screaming, Chad carried him toward the parking lot. By the time she joined them, they were both sulking in their seats. She suppressed a smile as she opened the rear of the SUV.

Chad got out and helped her put the grocery bags inside.

"How's it goin'?"

"Let's just say I'm ready to go home."

He looked as if he had worked a long tough twelve-hour shift.

She chuckled and patted him on the arm. "It's still a win."

He started the SUV. "Yeah, but that doesn't mean I'm taking a victory lap."

A few hours later, Izzy glanced at Chad as they made the short walk to the neighborhood park. He carried the casserole dish with the macaroni and cheese in it while she pushed the stroller with Henry strapped in the seat. She brushed a few strands of her hair away from her face as she carried on a conversation with Henry.

A group of Chad's neighbors greeted them with smiles and calls, each giving her inquiring looks. What must they think? That she was Chad's girlfriend? For some reason that idea didn't bother her when it should have.

Henry twisted around to look at Chad. "I swing?"

Chad looked at the group of children playing nearby. He nodded. "In a few minutes." Chad directed her toward a table loaded with food.

Izzy walked beside him. "I've not been to something like this in years."

"They didn't have these where you used to live?"

"We had them, but Richard didn't ever want

to go. No matter how many times I asked, nothing made him change his mind." She should have seen the signs. Maybe she just hadn't wanted to. It had always been a battle to get Richard to go with her anywhere. Why hadn't she stood up for what she wanted?

Chad pursed his lips. "I have to admit, this isn't my usual thing either. A couple of neighbors pretty much forced me to get out and come last year. I was glad I did and Henry enjoys the other children."

"Thanks for encouraging me to attend. I need to meet all the people I can." Izzy took the food from him and arranged the bowl on the table among the others.

"Your mac and cheese really looks good. I'm looking forward to eating some."

Warmth flowed through her. This time she met his look. He returned it and her heart did a little jump for joy.

They mingled with the others there. Chad introduced her to those he knew. A number they both met for the first time. As they moved around to different groups, Izzy spoke to Henry, keeping him happy. When it was time to eat, Izzy stood in the food line with Henry and Chad. She held Henry's plate while Chad placed food on it and filled his own plate at the same time. She managed to put food on hers as well. Chad spooned a double helping of her mac and cheese on his plate. He made sure he had her attention and winked as he scooped the second large spoonful.

She grinned like a girl whose crush had just proved he felt the same way as she did. Tomorrow she would worry about how tangled in Chad's charm she had become. Today she was going to enjoy having a handsome, smart, caring and funny man trying to impress her. It was an ointment to her burned self-esteem.

They were sharing a private moment. The spot in the center of her chest warmed. She liked Chad too much. With him, she recognized what she had missed in her life while being with Richard. It was nice to share humor and laughter again. Sadly she'd not had that for so long she'd failed to miss it. Chad had a very serious profession and being a single father had its challenges. Still, he could find joy in life. It was contagious.

With their plates filled, Chad's to overflowing, they found an empty park table. Henry sat between her and Chad. Izzy scooted in beside the boy and put an arm around him so he wouldn't fall backward off the picnic table bench. Chad settled Henry's plate in front of him and then took his spot close on the other side, sitting on the tips of her fingers. Heat ran up her neck. She quickly moved her hand.

Chad gave her a grin as his eyes twinkled. He leaned close. "Are you trying to touch my butt?"

"No!"

He grinned. "I wouldn't have minded."

She huffed and focused on her food.

Soon, an older couple took the bench across the table from them. Two children a few years older than Henry were with them.

"Hello," the woman said. "May we join you?"

"Sure," Chad agreed.

"I'm John Cartwright." The man offered his hand to Chad. "This is my wife, Elenore, and a couple of our grandchildren. We live over on Maple Street."

"It's nice to meet you. I'm Chad McCain. This is Izzy Lane and Henry." Chad placed his hand on Henry's head briefly. "We live over off of Lemon Drive."

"Hello," Izzy offered before Henry drew her attention away when he needed help.

"This is our first neighborhood get-together. We just moved here a few months ago," Mrs. Cartwright said.

"Welcome to the neighborhood," Chad offered.

"This is a nice idea." Mr. Cartwright nodded toward the food table. "Brings the neighborhood closer. That doesn't happen enough."

Over the next few minutes, their table settled into eating their meal.

Mrs. Cartwright smiled at Izzy. "We sat at the right table. You're such a lovely family."

"We're—" Izzy and Chad said at the same time.

The Cartwrights looked from Chad to Izzy and back again with confusion on their faces.

Chad cleared his throat. "Izzy is a coworker and rents an apartment from me. We're not married."

The Cartwrights faces cleared with understanding.

The man said, "We thought by the way you interacted with each other you were married. Sorry for the misunderstanding."

It shouldn't have bothered Izzy that they weren't a couple, but she couldn't deny the niggling feeling that it might be nice if they were. When had she started thinking like that? Before she met Chad, she'd been so determined to keep to herself, not share her history. Then the next thing she knew she was telling Chad the whole ugly story. What was happening to her?

A commotion at a table nearby drew her attention away from the uncomfortable moment.

A woman stood beside a small boy with a frantic look on her face. "Johnny, what's wrong?"

"I can't breathe," he gasped.

"Someone call 911." Chad climbed off the bench and loped toward them.

Izzy grabbed her phone. She explained where they were and what was happening.

In the background she heard Chad say, "I'm a doctor. Can I help?"

"He was just eating dessert and now he's got this rash and says he can't breathe." Panic filled the woman's voice.

Izzy said to the Cartwrights, "Can you watch Henry for me?"

They nodded.

She went around the table and handed Henry to Mrs. Cartwright. "Do you have an EpiPen?" Izzy asked the Cartwrights.

"I do." Mrs. Cartwright handed Henry back to Izzy before searching her purse. "One of the girls is allergic to everything."

Just before Izzy reached Chad he called, "Does anyone have an EpiPen?"

"Here's one." Izzy handed it over his shoulder.

Chad looked at her with surprise and appreciation. He took the pin. "That was quick."

"Hi, I'm Izzy," she said to the boy, directing his attention away from what Chad was about to do. "I'm a nurse and I can promise you'll feel better in a few minutes. Dr. McCain is going to make a quick prick and you'll be breathing easier."

Moving the boy's shorts to expose his thigh, Chad pushed the pin into his thigh.

Slowly the boy's color improved and his breathing eased. Izzy stood with the mother as Chad took the boy's vitals.

At the sound of an ambulance drawing near, Izzy said, "I'll go meet them."

Chad nodded.

Moments later she directed the EMTs to where the boy sat on the picnic table bench. As the EMTs went to work, Izzy and Chad joined the mother, who watched.

Chad spoke to her. "He needs to go to the hospital to be checked out. He's had an allergic reaction to something. Peanuts are the usual culprits, but it can be other things."

Fifteen minutes later the EMTs loaded the boy in the ambulance as Chad and Izzy stood nearby.

"Thank you," the mother called over her shoulder as she headed for her car.

"Where's Henry?" Chad made a frantic glance around as if he had just remembered him.

Izzy touched his arm. "He's with the Cartwrights. He's fine."

Chad relaxed. "Where did you come up with an EpiPen that quick?"

"Mrs. Cartwright. I figured there was a good chance that it would be needed."

They started back to their table.

"I'm impressed. I knew you were good but not how good." He put his arm around her shoulders and gave her a hug.

Chad's praise warmed her through and through like a roaring fire on a cold winter day. Another thing she hadn't known she needed until he came along. Someone to appreciate her.

Returning home at dusk with Izzy beside him and Henry asleep in the stroller had a rightness to it. Chad had never experienced that peace even during the best part of his marriage. In an odd way he had started thinking of the three of them as a family today. Something that he shouldn't continue to do.

He had no desire to lead Izzy on. He had accepted long ago that he hadn't been a good husband to Nan. That married life wasn't for him. Izzy wasn't a good-time girl who would expect nothing from a man. If anything, she would demand and deserve his best. He hadn't been able to give that before and wasn't confident he could do it now. Yet something about Izzy pulled at him. Challenged him. Made him want to tease her. Kiss her.

He couldn't believe how quickly Izzy had slipped into his life and fit. It should've scared him how much they looked like a family as they joined the others at the gathering earlier. For the first time in a long time, he'd felt positive about life. Chad had no intention of going into a serious relationship again, but if he had, Izzy would be the type of woman he'd choose to do it with. Still, his fear of not measuring up held him back.

Chad suspected he might be putting off his need for companionship on Izzy. She was nice and convenient. But also he couldn't ignore the sparks between them. Ones he'd never felt before.

"Well, thanks for inviting me. I have to say it was more exciting than I'd expected," Izzy said when they reached his drive.

"Yeah, not all of it was what I had expected either. I had planned on it being a little more low-key."

She shifted the empty bowl from one hand

to the other. She grinned. "That's hard to imagine. There's nothing low-key about you."

"I'm not sure if that's a compliment or not." Chad smiled like a guy who had been noticed by the prettiest girl in class.

The back porch light burned warm and inviting as they walked up the drive. Izzy had flipped it on as they went out his back door before going to the party. She'd said, "I hate coming home in the dark."

He was used to doing that. Even when Nan had been alive, she hadn't anticipated him coming home by doing something as simple as turning a light on.

Henry woke. "Izzy tuck me in?" His looked questioned her.

Izzy hesitated a moment. "Sure, I can do that."

She held the door for Chad to carry Henry into the house. He continued down the hall. A few moments later, she joined him in Henry's room minus the dirty dish.

In the process of removing Henry's clothes, Chad quickly slipped pajamas on the boy with the ease of practice. Henry laid in his bed and Chad pulled the covers up.

"I want Izzy," Henry whined.

Chad stood and Izzy came to sit on the bed beside Henry. She adjusted the blanket across his chest and kissed him on the forehead. "Night, sweet boy. Sleep tight. Now close your eyes."

Henry did as she asked.

Izzy stayed for a few minutes, then slipped out of the room. Had her eyes been glassy with moisture?

Chad returned to the kitchen to find Izzy sitting at the table with a mug of tea in front of her. Her eyes were clear. Maybe he had imagined those tears. "Hey there. Is Henry asleep?"

"Yeah. I appreciate you coming to tuck him in. I think he misses the female touch."

"I'm sure he does, but you're a great father. He loves you. I hope you don't mind, but I made myself at home. I needed a cup of tea."

Maybe she had been upset. "You're welcome anytime…" Chad paused. "I just don't know that I'm enough for him."

"I'm sure there are many parents who feel like that. That's how life works."

Chad pulled a drink out of the refrigerator. "You make it all sound okay."

She twisted her mug. "I didn't mean to belittle your troubles."

"I didn't think you were." He took a seat beside her at the table.

"I think we were the talk of the picnic in more ways than one today."

Chad groaned. She giggled. He studied her a moment.

"What?" Her brows rose.

"I like that sound."

"Sound?" Izzy looked around the room.

"You giggling. It's like windchimes ringing."

She shyly dipped her head. "Thank you. You keep saying such nice things. Flattery will get you everywhere."

He raised one eyebrow in suggestion. "Everywhere? I like the idea of that."

She offered him a smirky grin. "You know what I meant. By the way, I've been meaning to tell you that I won't be here next weekend. I need to go to my parents' and pick up the furniture stored there. They're ready to get it out of their way and I could use it."

"What're your plans to haul it here?" Chad stretched out his legs, getting comfortable.

"I'm still thinking about that. I'm either going to rent a truck or drive my father's back down. I hate to do that though. He uses it almost daily. It'll put him in a bind to have to ride around in my tiny car."

Chad winced. "I can imagine that would be uncomfortable."

She looked him up and down, "I guess you could."

It gave him a particular feeling in his lower half to have her study him as if she missed nothing. "It's small."

She laughed. "You'd look like one of those clowns in a circus car getting out of mine."

He chuckled. "But it's just the right size and looks good on you."

Izzy's face went a pretty shade of pink. Had she never been told how attractive she was? That guy she'd given so much of her life to had been a real jerk.

"Instead of renting or borrowing a truck, why don't Henry and I just go with you? I could rent a trailer up there and tow your stuff back. Get it all in one trip. How does that sound?"

She fiddled with her mug as if unsure of that idea. "Let me think about it."

"What's there to think about? I have the weekend off and you do too. If I'm out of town, I can get all my time. You told me I need to make the most of my time."

"Yeah, but I didn't mean by driving up and down the road for me."

"Henry and I, plus you, will get to spend some quality time together." He took a swallow of his drink.

She moved her head from one side to the other in thought. "I guess we could. It would be nice to get it all in one trip. But I hate to ask you for such a big favor."

"But you didn't ask. I offered." For some reason he really wanted to do this for her. To spend time getting to know her better. Going down the road would certainly give him a chance to do that.

"Let me talk to my parents and get back to you." She stood. "I better go. I have to be in early in the morning."

"I'm on the night shift." He picked up her mug and put it in the sink.

Izzy stepped to the door. "That's always fun."

"At least when we're busy, time goes by fast." He stepped toward her. "I'll walk you home."

"Not necessary. I'm just out back. I think I can make it." She waved a hand for him to stay there.

Chad's gaze filled with heat captured hers. "I know right where you are, and I'd still like to make sure you get home."

They made their way along the path to her door. Chad placed a hand on her upper arm, stopping her before she went inside. "Izzy, I know it might not be a good idea but I'd very much like to kiss you. But you can tell me no. Stop me if you don't want it."

Chad waited. She said nothing, then took a small step toward him. His heart picked up speed as his hands circled both her upper arms, holding her with a light touch. He looked into her eyes as his lips touched hers. Her mouth was warm and responsive as he teased her plump bottom lip. Izzy tasted so inviting. She returned his actions sending his heart rate into overdrive. The blood roared in his ears as his desire grew.

Letting his fingers travel down her arms to her waist, he nudged her against him. Her arms slid up his chest to wrap around his neck. He deepened the kiss and she joined him, a moan slipping from her lips. He ran the tip of his tongue along the seam of her mouth, asking for entrance.

To his delight, she opened for him. Her hands went to his shoulders, gripping them. Chad held himself in check with an effort not to crush her against him. He could overwhelm her, cause her to bolt. His desire could get out of hand. He eased back.

Izzy moved against him as if wanting all he could give. He had plenty to share. His arm tightened around her waist as his other hand ran along her rib cage. His thumb brushed the curve of her breast. The mewing sounds from

Izzy heightened his need. He demanded more. She gave it.

The neighbor's back porch light blinked on. Izzy jerked away from him, and he said a sharp word under his breath She looked everywhere but at him. This wasn't what he wanted. Not at all.

"I'm sorry. I shouldn't have let you do that. Please forget it happened." With that, she went inside and didn't look back.

Hell would freeze over before he forgot that red-hot kiss.

CHAPTER FIVE

EARLY THE NEXT Saturday morning, Izzy sat in the front passenger seat of Chad's SUV while he drove. Henry was securely strapped in his car seat behind them, chatting happily about everything he saw out the windows. Izzy joined him in looking through the windshield into the bright sunshine.

Chad had spoken to her again in the middle of the week while they were at work and convinced her he and Henry should drive her to her parents'. Regardless of her serious reservation about agreeing, she couldn't disagree with his logic. To her dismay but not surprise, her parents had insisted Chad and Henry spend the night with them. Izzy's middle fluttered with nerves. It looked like there was more to her and Chad's relationship than she'd intended. Her intention had been to pick up the furniture she had stored and return the next day. Not give her parents ideas.

After Chad's kiss, it was difficult not to have ideas of her own. She'd spent most of the week trying to forget about it. Unsuccessfully. About how it made her feel. How she had clung to him. How she had wanted him to do it again.

Then the denial came. She couldn't let it happen again. It was too important she protect herself. Think rationally. To not be naive. For self-preservation's sake, she couldn't get into another relationship. She couldn't afford emotionally to misjudge a man again. What she wanted and needed had to matter as much to the man as it did to her.

When Henry settled down and then slept, Chad said, "It's nice of your mom and dad to invite Henry and me to spend the night at their house."

Izzy lips tightened. "That's the kind of people they are. They'll welcome anybody." Izzy's eyes widened, realizing how callous she'd just sounded. "I'm sorry. I didn't mean for that to sound the way it did. I should have said they're very hospitable."

"If you'd be more comfortable, I'll get Henry and me a hotel room."

"No, no." She shook her head. "Don't do that. Mom wouldn't be happy if you did. I appreciate you going to this much trouble for me.

I'm sure this isn't the way you wanted to spend your weekend off."

"Hey, I'm glad to get out of town. It's been a while since I've had an entire weekend off and I want every minute of it."

"The life of a doctor," she quipped.

Chad glanced at her with a shadow of gloom in his eyes. Had he thought of his wife's attitude about his job? "Glamorous, isn't it?"

They both laughed, which broke the tension she'd been feeling. Those simple moments let her slip back into the easy way between them.

"Why did you become a doctor?" Izzy suddenly wanted to know what made him who he was.

"I wished I could say it was an earth-shattering moment, a lightning bolt from the sky or some tragedy. But it was more like I was good at math and science and my teachers encouraged me to think about being a doctor. I decided to go to med school and found my home. I love the science of the job but most of all I love the patients. They come to me needing help and I give it to them. I help make lives different in the middle of heartbreak. There's little in the world more rewarding than that."

Wow. Izzy studied him a moment. She wasn't supposed to let him draw her further under his spell, but somehow he'd managed to make it happen.

"I don't think just being good in math and science was the only reason you went into medicine. I've seen you in action. You have the smarts and the capacity for empathy. Don't deny it. I've seen you talk to parents. They feel you care. That's what makes you one of the best doctors I've ever worked with."

Chad moved his hand as if fanning himself. He grinned. "Stop. You're embarrassing me." He glanced at her. "Not much different than the life of a nurse I would imagine."

"Not much." She checked on Henry, who still slept. "Aw, but the life of a child."

"You're welcome to take a nap. You don't have to entertain me." Chad had them moving down the road at a steady speed.

Izzy looked at his strong profile. This morning he hadn't shaved. Dark stubble covered his jaw, giving him a ruggish look she found appealing. "I'll be glad to drive as well. Let you nap if you want."

He changed lanes. "I'm a little old-school when it comes to driving."

She couldn't decide if she was impressed or not. "It comes with the macho-man image, doesn't it?"

Chad's brows drew together. "I've never considered myself a macho man."

"You qualify in my book." She sucked in a breath. That she shouldn't have said. It was too telling about how she felt about him. Truthfully nothing between them could be called just friendly any longer. The air around them sizzled when they were together. Like now, in this small space, sparks popped as if embers from a fire floating into a night sky.

She had to accept that. What simmered between them was desire. Two adults who wanted each other in the most basic way. There wasn't anything wrong with that. Would it be so bad to act on their attraction? If she held her heart in check.

A big goofy grin spread across Chad's lips. "Thank you, ma'am."

"Don't get any ideas," she huffed. "That sort of slipped out."

"Doesn't matter how it got out. I'll take it as a compliment." He smiled.

She looked out the side window and said flatly, "Maybe it isn't. It all depends on how you define macho man."

The grin left his face and his eyes turned serious. "And how would you define it?"

Confident she didn't want to go into all the positive attributes she saw in him, she had to redirect his question. "You know this conversation isn't going in a direction that I'm completely comfortable with."

His silvery eyes twinkled. "I was rather enjoying it."

"I can tell. It was all about you."

He chuckled. "Of course, we could discuss you."

"I don't particularly like that subject either." Chad had to already think she was pitiful after she'd told him how she let a man walk all over her.

"Tell me about your family then. Your mom and dad. What to expect."

Izzy leaned back in the seat, turning her back to the door slightly so she could see him more clearly. "I guess they're like anybody else's parents. They raised three children. They live in a subdivision in a brick ranch house like the others around them."

"And in this idyllic life, did you have a dog?" A humorous note filled his question along with a seriousness. He really sounded like he wanted to know.

"Yep. Leon. I named him after my first boyfriend."

"Interesting." Chad nodded as if he were a sociologist learning something important about her. "Makes me worry about your next dog's name."

She laughed, something she did a lot around Chad. "I thought it fit. Anyway, Dad is retired. Mom still teaches school. She is thinking about retirement next year."

"And how about your siblings?"

"You are full of questions. I have one sister. She lives in Memphis with her husband and three children. My brother lives in Nashville and has a wife and son and a baby on the way. You may meet him tonight. He usually makes an appearance when I come home."

Her plans had been to have the same thing as the rest of her family. A happy marriage, children and a life with someone special. But she'd failed. Instead she helped put Richard through school, which now made her sick to her stomach to think about. All that time and money and emotion wasted. She had fallen for Richard's promises of tomorrow that had turned into years of nothing—used and betrayed.

"What're you thinking?"

"How do you know I'm thinking anything? Aren't your eyes supposed to be on the road?"

"You got quiet, and your mouth pursed." He stated this with confidence.

Chad already knew her better than Richard

ever had. Oddly that comforted her. She relaxed her facial muscles. "I don't purse."

He gave her a quick speculative glance. "If you say so but it sure looked as if you did. Regardless of that, what's bothering you?"

"I was just thinking about how happy my brother and sister are." She wasn't lying.

"And you wish you had what they do, don't you?"

Apparently she was completely transparent where Chad was concerned.

"Look, we all make mistakes. Heaven knows, I certainly have." He glanced over his shoulder to Henry. "But sometimes we have to go through the muck to come out on the other side on dry land and for the better. Along the way we must remember we're worthy of happiness."

She wiped her cheek. "Why, Dr. McCain, I had no idea you were so philosophical."

"Not philosophical so much as a man who saw his life turning out differently. You had a jerk for a boyfriend. Now you don't. It's time to leave that all behind you and live again."

"Like you are?"

"I'm trying. Some days are easier than others. Other days I have my boots stuck in the muck just like everyone else. But I do try to keep pulling them out."

* * *

Chad feared he'd gone too deep with Izzy. Been too hard on her. Had stepped too far into her personal life. But he wanted to know more about her. She said nothing after his little speech. A few minutes later, he'd looked over to find her eyes closed. Maybe he had added to her issues.

She'd told him to forget about their kiss. Like that was going to happen. Instead of forgetting it, he relived it over and over. It had been different than any kiss he'd ever experienced. It could only be because it was with Izzy. But that didn't mean he should pursue her further.

Hadn't he promised himself it would remain Henry and him against the world? Chad had thought about it and decided that was the best way not to have either one of their hearts broken. He knew well what a bad relationship could do to their lives, and he didn't intend to enter into another one again.

He wasn't going to offer Izzy any more than what they had now. Marriage would never enter his plans. He'd been poor at it the first time and he wouldn't take a chance on being in that situation again. Izzy deserved the best and he had proved he wasn't. What he needed to do was step carefully and not mislead Izzy into believing he could give more than he could.

Izzy woke as they approached the outskirts of Nashville. He'd had to work to concentrate on not going off the road as she stretched in the seat. "Sorry, I didn't mean to go to sleep on you."

Chad wished she had gone to sleep on him. Literally. Those visions did nothing to help him remain loyal to his vow to stay uninvolved with her.

Twisting, she looked between the seats and said to Henry, "Hey there. We're both sleepy-heads."

Chad watched through the rearview mirror as Henry returned Izzy's grin. She was so good with him. Chad shook his head. She should be, after all she was a pediatric nurse.

"I need some directions, Izzy." She told him which exit he needed to take off the interstate. As he pulled into the quaint suburban town outside of Nashville, he scanned the area. "This must have been a nice place to grow up."

"Yeah, it was. Most people who live here commute into Nashville or are part of the music industry."

"What did your dad do before he retired?"

"He was an executive with an insurance

company. Nashville's one of the biggest insurance centers in the nation."

"I had no idea. With an executive and a teacher as parents, what made you decide to become a nurse?"

"I always like helping people. My dolls, my dog, the girl down the street. It was a natural progression. I volunteered in the local hospital. One of the older nurses took me under her wing and encouraged me to go to nursing school. I worked and went to school at the same time. Richard just went to school." She didn't try to keep the bitterness out of her voice.

"You mean you supported him and went to school at the same time?" What would it be like to have that type of devotion in his life? The more he knew about Izzy, the more he admired her.

"I did. Sort of stupid, wasn't I?"

"I was thinking you were pretty amazing. I wish my wife had shown that amount of love and support." A sadness surrounded his words.

"That's nice of you to say, but I should have recognized when I was being taken for a ride. Being used."

"Love makes us put on blinders sometimes. I knew Nan wasn't happy, but I wanted to keep it together for Henry."

"Yeah, but that's different. I worked while

Richard went to school. First his undergraduate degree, then his master's. All the time we talked about getting married. Or come to think of it, I talked about marriage. He would say *let me get through school and get the right job.* Then it was *until I get this or that promotion.* What type of person keeps believing that?"

Chad took her hand. He liked that she didn't pull away. "The type that believes in people. Wants to see the best in them. The kind of person who has a big heart and wants to help people. There's nothing wrong with you. All that was on him. You have nothing to beat yourself up over."

"You sure know how to make a person feel better." She offered him a wry smile.

"Just part of my charm. Or more like been there, done that."

She laughed. He returned it. At least Izzy didn't look as sad as she had earlier.

Izzy grew tense the closer they came to her parents' house. When Chad's hand returned to the steering wheel, she placed hers in her lap. She began clasping and unclasping her hands. "You need to take the next right into that subdivision."

Chad followed her directions. "Are you nervous about seeing your parents? Or about them meeting Henry and me?"

"You would notice." Izzy looked out the side window.

"It's pretty hard to miss."

She sighed and looked at him. "Let's just say my mom and dad will make more of you being with me than they should."

"Why is that?" He slowly drove down the street.

"They never liked Richard and they'll see you as a nice replacement."

His brows rose. "They don't even know me."

"You're not Richard." She paused. Chad was so much better. In so many ways. "And I might have told them a few things about you."

"Like how well my son behaves in the grocery store?" He grinned.

Izzy laughed. She liked that Chad could laugh at himself. "I might have left that out. Even if I never said anything, it wouldn't have mattered because they'd like any kind of replacement."

"That doesn't sound like a ringing endorsement. They disliked Richard that much?"

Her mouth tightened. She had said things she didn't want to. "They saw through him far earlier than I did."

Chad continued to drive along the tree-lined streets filled with large older homes. It reminded her of the area she now lived in but hillier. No wonder she was pleased with her apartment. She clasped her hands once more.

He placed his hand over hers. "Hey, everything's going to be fine."

"You'll think that until you get tangled up in whatever my parents will say and do."

"What'll they do or say?" Chad's face screwed up in confusion.

"Ask personal questions. Make embarrassing suggestions. Assumptions." Her words came out in a flood. She didn't want Chad embarrassed. Or worse to feel pressured to feel something for her.

"I think I can handle anything they come up with. Don't worry."

"Just remember you've been warned." She looked ahead. "It's the house down on the right with the two big oaks in the front yard."

"I see it." He swung the SUV into the paved drive.

Her parents exited the front door the second Chad stopped the car. Had they been looking out the window for them?

Despite Izzy's concerns, she hopped out of the SUV and hurried toward them. She loved them dearly. They just wanted her to be happy.

Chad was in the process of lifting Henry

out of the car seat when Izzy and her parents came to stand on the lawn nearby. He closed the door, turned to the group with a smile. He held Henry in his arms.

"Mom and Dad—" Izzy moved to stand between him and her parents "—this is Chad McCain and his son, Henry. Chad is my landlord and coworker." She gave Henry a reassuring smile.

"It's a pleasure to meet you, sir." Chad extended a hand to Izzy's father. He took it with a firm grip.

Izzy moaned inwardly when her mother pulled Chad into a hug with Henry between them.

"It's nice to meet you as well." Her mother let Chad go and stepped back. "I understand you've been very good to Izzy."

This time Izzy's groan was loud enough that Chad looked at her with a grin. "I've tried but I have to admit she's done more for Henry and me than we have for her."

Izzy's mom looked at Henry. "Hi, Henry. I'm Martha. I just made a batch of cookies and I wondered if you'd help me eat them."

Henry's eyes opened wide. He looked at Chad, who smiled. "You can have some."

Izzy was impressed with how Chad and

Henry interacted, and without Henry screaming a demand.

Her mother put out her hands. "Why don't
you come with me? We'll go get a big glass
of milk and have a few cookies. You can call
me Mama Lane. That's what my grandchildren call me."

"What about me?" Izzy's father asked. "I
like cookies too."

Henry had willingly gone with her mother.
They started toward the front door. Over her
shoulder her mother said, "Izzy, you show
Chad where to put his bags. He and Henry
will be staying in the back room with the twin
beds. You take your old room."

Izzy and Chad stood watching the older couple completely engrossed in what Henry was
telling them. They shared a laugh.

She nudged Chad. "You probably don't
know it but that'll be the last you see Henry
until we leave if they give him back then."

Chad chuckled. "I figured that might be the
case. How're you holding up so far?"

Heat went to her cheeks. "I'm okay. I'll get
through it. By the way, you and Henry did
great a minute ago about the cookies. I was
impressed."

"I can't take all the credit. It was from your
good example. Even Ms. Weber has com-

mented on the difference. She's been telling me for months I should do something."

Izzy couldn't help but be proud. "I'm glad you think I've helped."

"I want you to know that I won't take anything your parents say to heart." He removed their bags from the SUV and started toward the house.

She joined him. "I'm counting on that."

Izzy led the way inside, then to the bedrooms. She took her bag and placed it in her room across the hall from where Chad and Henry would be staying. Then they followed the sound of Henry's laughter to the kitchen. He was obviously entertaining her parents. She and Chad found them all sitting around a kitchen bar, eating cookies.

"Any chance I could get one of those?" Chad asked.

Izzy's mother quickly gathered a plate and a cup of coffee. She placed them in front of him at the bar.

"Thank you, Mrs. Lane. Please don't feel like you must wait on us while we're here."

"I promise I'm not doing for you any more than I would for anybody else." She glanced toward Izzy.

"She's not kidding." Izzy took a cookie and bit into it. "These are great as usual, Mom. I hate to run out just as soon as we got here but I made arrangements to rent a trailer. We're gonna need to go get it before the place closes. I want to have time to load things ahead of when it gets dark. We must be headed back first thing in the morning."

"Can't you stay longer?" her mother whined.

"Not this time. It'll be longer next, I promise, Mom."

"Why don't you let Henry stay here with us while y'all go and pick up the trailer? We'll find something fun to do," her mother offered.

"That's fine with me. If you're sure?" Chad looked from her mother to her father, who nodded.

Chad turned to Henry. "Would you like to stay here and play with toys until I get back in a little while?"

"Toys?" Henry gave an eager nod.

They all laughed.

"I'll expect you to behave." Chad's look turned stern.

"We better go," Izzy said, touching Chad's shoulder.

Izzy noticed her mother watching them closely.

"I'm ready." Chad stood.

Mr. Lane did as well. "I appreciate you helping Izzy out this way. She's got that tiny car that doesn't hold anything to speak of."

Izzy put her arm around her father's waist and hugged him. "Tell the truth. What you're glad of is not having to give up your pickup truck for a couple of weeks."

"That too." Her father pulled her tighter.

Later that evening Izzy sat back in her chair at her parents' dining room table, listening as Chad kept up a running conversation with her parents. Her brother, Steve, and his wife, Laura, who had come for dinner, joined in the discussion. Chad fit into her family perfectly. Even Henry enjoyed playing with her nephew, Ross, despite being younger.

Richard had never melded with her family during the few times he had visited her parents. In fact he struggled with any kind of relationship with her parents as well as her siblings. As the years went by, Richard joined her less and less when she came home. He always found excuses to stay behind. In contrast, Chad, who barely knew them, acted like an old friend.

"Martha, I can certainly tell where Izzy got her culinary skills." Chad sighed with satisfaction. "That might be one of the best meals I've ever had."

Izzy watched her mother preen under his

praise. Even if Chad laid it on a little thick, Izzy appreciated his efforts. It was important to her mom for people to appreciate her cooking.

"Thank you, Chad. Feel free to flatter me anytime." Her mother smiled brightly.

Chad laughed and so did the rest at the table. "May I help you clean up?"

"My goodness, no. My guests don't help clean the table. Instead, why don't you young folks go into Nashville and see what's going on."

Steve and Laura looked at each other and shook their heads. Laura said, "I'm sorry. I wish we could but it's already past bedtime for Ross." She grinned and patted her rounded middle. "And for me and this new little one on the way."

"We'll watch Henry," her mom stated as she looked at Izzy, then Chad. "So that you can go."

Izzy narrowed her eyes at her mother. "Mom, I don't think Chad wants to do that. He's driven up here and then loaded the trailer. He may be too tired to go out."

She'd helped as much as she could with the loading of her belongings onto the trailer, but Chad with her father's help had done the bulk of the work. A couple of times she'd caught herself watching Chad's muscles ripple beneath his shirt as he lifted the furniture. Heat had flashed up her neck to her cheeks when he caught her doing so. He'd grinned and winked as if he knew she'd been ogling him. She'd quickly made herself busy, directing her father to the next piece of furniture to load. Chad was far too perceptive for the stability of her nerves.

"I can't impose by leaving Henry here. It wasn't my intent to come and put him off on you."

"We wouldn't mind. You two go enjoy yourselves. If you've never been to Broadway or by the Parthenon at night, you should. You can drive my car since the SUV has the trailer on it."

Izzy sighed. Her mother had thought of everything. Pulling out all the stops to let her and Chad have some time alone. Without making too much of a scene, Izzy didn't know how to stop the forward motion of her mother in train-engine mode.

"Go on." Her mother waved a hand. "Chad said he's never been to Nashville except passing through."

Izzy gave Chad a questioning look. He quirked his lip as he shrugged. "Sounds like fun if your parents are sure they don't mind watching Henry."

"We don't mind at all," her mother jumped to answer. "Why don't we get Henry ready for bed and settled before you go. Then you won't have to be worried about him being any trouble."

"He's had a big day so he should go right to sleep." Chad pushed back from the table.

"While you do that, I'll help Mom with the dishes and cleaning up." Izzy gathered the dirty plates within reach.

"All right. I'll meet you at the front door in twenty minutes." Chad went in search of Henry, who was playing with Ross in the den. Steve and Laura gathered their things to leave.

Steve gave Izzy a hug. "Chad's a nice guy. Way better than that other one."

Izzy shook her head. "There's nothing between us. He's just my landlord."

"I've never seen a landlord look at someone the way he does you." Her brother's eyes twinkled.

Laura joined him. "Come to think of it, I never have either."

Her brother put his arm around Izzy's shoulders and squeezed. "Nope, he likes you."

Izzy swatted at his chest. "Enough of that."

"It's great to see you. We miss you around

here, but I understand why you felt you needed to move." Steve put his arm around her shoulder.

"I'll come home when I can. You guys can always come visit me." Izzy hugged him, then Laura.

"We'll try to do that soon," Laura assured Izzy while rubbing her stomach. "Give us time to get this girl here."

They hustled out of the house, taking Ross with them as he complained about having to leave.

Izzy joined her mom in the kitchen. She shooed Izzy out. "Why don't you go freshen up your face? Maybe change your shirt for something sweeter before y'all head out."

"Mom, I've told you more than once that Chad and I are just friends."

"Okay, so you don't think you need to look nice even for a friend. Or anybody else you might meet?" She gave Izzy a nudge. "Go on and do what your mother says. You'll be glad you did."

Knowing she wouldn't win the argument, Izzy took her mother's advice. Izzy pulled on a ruffled blouse and let her hair down, giving it a good brushing. She then checked on Chad and Henry.

"Izzy tuck in?"

"Sure, honey," she answered before Chad could say anything.

Sitting on the side of the bed, she kissed Henry on the forehead. "Good night. Sleep tight. See you in the morning."

She stood. Chad took her spot. "I'll be there in a few minutes."

Chad soon joined her in the living room.

Izzy wasn't comfortable having her parents force Chad to spend time with her. "You know we don't have to go out. We don't have to do this just because my mother insisted."

His look held hers. "I'm a grown man. I know I can make my own decisions. I'd like to go if you would."

Izzy plastered a smile on her face. If he wanted to do this, then so did she. "Come on then. Let's go see what Nashville has to offer."

An hour later Izzy strolled beside Chad as they moved down Broadway. "This is the older section of Nashville. The area known for honky-tonks and music cafés. Many of the country music singers got their start here. I'm sure you've heard Nashville is the capital of country music."

"Yes. That much I do know." Chad took her hand as the crowd grew larger around them.

She left her hand there, not wanting them

to get separated. At least that's what she told herself. It felt natural to have Chad's hand surrounding hers.

"Go on. I'm enjoying having my own personal tour guide."

Izzy appreciated how effortlessly Chad built up her ego. It had been so damaged by Richard it was wonderful to have someone who treated her with respect. "The Bluebird Café, just around the corner, is known for launching many famous performers. They still host up-and-comers today. I don't know if we can get in, but we can try."

"That's all right. Country music isn't my favorite, but I certainly listen to a lot of crossover artists."

"We could go to the Wild Horse Saloon and have a drink. It's just over there." She pointed across the street. "How're you at line dancing?"

"We can if you want to."

For once Chad sounded unsure. "That sounded less than enthusiastic."

"Ah, come on. I'll try anything once." He gave her hand a tug.

She smiled. "Anything?"

An intensity filled his eyes. "Almost anything."

A shiver went through her. She had the idea they might not be talking about the same thing.

They entered a large two-story room that was filled with people. The dance floor was already busy. They found a small table along the back wall and ordered a drink.

"So." Chad gave the dance floor a doubtful look. "Have you done much line dancing?"

"I've done my share. Few people live in Nashville and don't line dance or listen to country music. I even own a pair of cowboy boots. They're tucked away in the back of my closet."

He wiggled his brows. "I like a girl in boots."

Izzy grinned. "Are you flirting with me?"

"Maybe a little bit." He grinned. "Do you mind?"

She dipped her head, aware of the warmth coursing through her. "Not really."

They sipped their drinks through a couple songs.

Izzy was interested to see what skills Chad had in the dancing department. He seemed flawless in all she'd ever seen him do. "You ready to give it a try?"

Chad held out a hand, palm up. "If you promise not to make fun of me."

His boyish look of worry pulled at her heart-strings. She placed her hand in his. "I'll be there right beside you. Just follow what the others are doing."

They went to the dance floor, forming a straight line along with everybody else. Just as she suspected, Chad caught on quickly and was quite a good dancer. She watched him move to the music, his actions lithe and sure. His dips were particularly nice because she had a chance to appreciate the grip of his jeans across his butt. Best of all, he acted as if he was having fun. The fact he had been willing to try something new was refreshing. She appreciated that he didn't take himself too seriously. Something Richard couldn't do.

They danced for another half hour before Chad said close to her ear. "It's time for me to sit down. I haven't had this type of physical activity in a long time."

Izzy led the way back to their table, but it had been cleaned and taken by another couple. "What do you say to slowing the music down? There's a piano bar farther down the street that I've heard is really good."

Chad again spoke next to her ear, the brush of his words going across her cheek like a caress. She shivered. "It sounds like a good plan."

They soon found the small dark club that looked like little more than a dive. A female voice sang a Patsy Cline song as they found a table in the dark room with a piano located in the middle. A few couples circled a small dance floor off to the side.

Izzy leaned across the table. "It's still pretty early so there aren't a lot of people here yet."

A girl came to take their drink order and they settled in to listen.

"She really has a good voice." Chad nodded toward the piano player.

Izzy smiled. "She is good."

The piano player started to sing a slow sultry song.

Chad stood and offered his hand. "This is more my speed. Would you care to dance?"

Izzy wasn't sure she should be so close to Chad, but she couldn't pass up the opportunity either. The idea of him holding her made her nerves quiver. She placed her fingers in his. He led her to the floor and confidently pulled her into his arms. Chad led her with poise and grace to the beat of the music. As they swayed, he placed his cheek against the top of her head. Slowly, he moved them around the floor.

Her hand stroked his shoulder. Could she stay here forever? Not an idea she should be entertaining.

"I'm glad your mom insisted we come down here," Chad whispered against her ear.

Izzy couldn't disagree.

They danced seamlessly into the next song. When that one ended, Chad said, "Wait right here." He went to the piano player and spoke to her before dropping some bills in a jar.

The lady glanced at them, then the notes of "Penny Lane" began to fill the room.

Izzy smiled and shook her head as Chad took her in his arms again, moving her into a faster step.

His lips brushed her temple on the way to her ear. "I couldn't resist."

"You know you've ruined this song for me forever. Every time I hear it, I'll think of you."

He held her gaze with those all-knowing eyes. "And that's a bad thing?"

It could be a heartbreaking one. She needed to change the subject.

Chad took her through a pattern of fancy steps.

"I thought you couldn't dance?" she panted, a little breathless.

"Never said I couldn't. Just that I've not done much line dancing."

Izzy smiled. "I think I've been had."

He grinned. "I like holding you much better than standing beside you."

She couldn't disagree with him. Finally left no choice, Izzy said, "It's getting late. You've had a long day. I better get you home."

Chad's gaze held hers. "Too bad. I was enjoying holding you."

Heat filled her. Could they have an uncomplicated relationship? She did enjoy his company. They headed toward the entrance. She felt Chad close behind her. As she exited to the sidewalk, Izzy bumped into someone.

"Hey!"

Her heart went to her throat. She knew that voice.

"I'm sorry," she murmured. The dreamy world she'd been in with Chad dissipated in a flash. She didn't need this now.

"Izzy."

Her hands trembled. Of all the people in the world she could run into, it had to be Richard!

She said his name as dry as a dessert plain. "Richard."

She felt more than saw Chad step close. Izzy appreciated his support. She straightened her shoulders, looking Richard in the eye. After all, she'd done nothing wrong. She refused to act as if she had. He's the one who should be ashamed.

"How're you?" Richard asked.

He acted as if they were old friends with nothing negative between them. "I'm fine."

An obviously pregnant woman came to stand next to Richard. Her hand curled around his arm, a wedding ring glimmering in the light. Izzy's heart tightened with disappointment, grief and resentment. This other woman had all that Richard had promised her. A marriage and a soon-to-be family. Izzy's supper turned in her stomach.

"I heard you moved to Atlanta."

"Yes. I'm home collecting the rest of my furniture." Why was she explaining herself to him?

Richard glanced at Chad.

Izzy felt no compunction to introduce the two men. She had no desire to contaminate Chad with someone like Richard. All she wanted was to get out of there. "We have to be going. Goodbye, Richard."

Chad wrapped a reassuring arm around her waist and led her away. "I guess that was Richard, the ex?"

"Yes."

Chad kept a hand at her waist as they headed to the parking lot. "Enough said."

Chad couldn't help but be impressed with Izzy's civil reaction to meeting her ex again after what he had done to her. If it had been him seeing Nan again, Chad wasn't sure he could have done as well. In fact, he was tempted to turn around and punch Richard for how he'd treated Izzy. What he was still doing to her. Their relationship had completely colored Izzy's view of the world.

Izzy said nothing on the way to the car. He kept his arm around her waist as they made their way down the crowded sidewalk. He didn't press her for more information. Instead he held her close even when he didn't need to. Her body remained ridged.

Inside the car she gave him directions in a subdued voice. It wasn't until they were close to her parents' house that Izzy said, "I'm sorry you had to witness that."

"You have nothing to be sorry about."

"We were having a nice evening, then my ugly baggage comes out of hiding." The words hissed through her clinched teeth.

"You had no control over that." He pulled over into the parking lot of a small park and turned off the car. "Do you want to talk about it? It might make you feel better."

Izzy stared out the windshield with her hands clasped in her lap. "We were together for nine years. We talked about getting married and starting a family. He acted as if he wanted it as much as I did. But there was always something in the way. Needing to finish school, finding a good enough job, him getting a certain promotion so we'd have the money.

There was always an excuse. Then one day eight months ago I come home to find him in bed with that woman." She all but spit out the word *that*. "Now she's pregnant. Having the baby that should have been mine. She has everything that Richard kept promising me." Izzy let out a little sob.

Chad's chest tightened, wanting to absorb her pain. "There'll be another man—a better man—and a houseful of children, I'm sure." Chad kept his voice low and reassuring. Who wouldn't want a woman as lovely as Izzy? The guy must be an idiot.

"I hope so. I just wish I hadn't wasted so much time on him. My sister and brother already have families. Then there's me, the odd man out."

"We all know I'm not a shining example of how to have the perfect relationship." That's why he didn't trust himself to ever consider marriage again. He couldn't afford to get it wrong again. He and Henry deserved the right person.

"Yeah, but I feel so stupid."

Chad smiled wryly. "I've been there and done that too." He took one of her hands and played with her fingers.

She looked at him. "What do we do about our bad choices?"

"It has been my experience you live and learn." Chad pulled her into a reassuring hug.

Izzy returned it. Her lips brushed his cheek and traveled toward his mouth. "You're a nice man," she whispered. "Not only did I drag you up here to get my furniture, but you put up with my parents' not-so-subtle matchmaking, then I involve you in my emotional baggage."

He chuckled. "You do know how to entertain a man."

"I know other ways to entertain." Her mouth found his.

Izzy's lips were plump, reminding him of berries warm from the summer sun. She opened in invitation, causing his blood to pulse through his veins. Her tongue searched for his. She sighed and pressed into him. Chad took over the kiss, applying more pressure as his hand traveled along her side and slipped under her satiny blouse to the silk of her skin. Izzy whimpered and rubbed against him.

He pulled her across the console dividing them until she sat in his lap. Her hip pressed into his stiff manhood. "Izzy."

She kissed along his jaw to nip at his earlobe.

The flash of headlights going by brought him back to reality. "I'm sure I'll hate myself for this later, but we need to think about what we're doing. As much as I'd enjoy having you right here and now, it's not the time or the place. I won't have you in the back seat of your mother's car. More importantly, I've no interest in being your rebound guy. I'd rather you not regret being with me."

Izzy went stock-still. Even in the dim light he could see her stricken look. As if she'd just realized what she was doing. He found that flattering.

"I'm, uh…sorry." With jerky movements, she pushed away from him. When she had difficulty getting over the console, he helped her. She scrambled the rest of the way into her seat.

"You have nothing to be sorry for."

Izzy said no more as he started the car and drove to her parents'. In the time it took him to climbed out of the car, Izzy was almost to the front door of the house. "Izzy."

She stopped and waited for him.

He joined her and his hands cupped her shoulders before he placed a kiss on her forehead. "Things will look better in the morning. I promise."

CHAPTER SIX

IZZY HAD TO force herself to face Chad the next morning at the breakfast table. She'd embarrassed herself on a level that was unprecedented. Had she actually thrown herself at him? She groaned. Was she really that desperate?

"Are you okay, honey?" her mother asked.

"I'm fine." She chanced a glance at Chad to find him giving her a reassuring smile. It eased some of her pain. Marginally. When had she become so desperate for attention that she would throw herself at a man?

Regardless of Chad's silent encouragement, she kept her eyes averted from his as much as possible. She could feel Chad watching her as she interacted with her parents and Henry.

Chad's rejection still stung even though he had a good reason for doing so. In an indescribable way, Chad's actions pained her more than Richard's had. She hadn't intended to put herself in that position again. After last night she intended to keep that distance she had originally believed she needed to have from Chad. Even a hint of not being wanted hurt. She had had enough of that in her life.

They left her parents' home with them smiling and chitchatting with Chad and Henry nonstop. They even had Chad agreeing to return for a visit soon. Just as she feared, her parents had become too friendly with Chad for her comfort. They wanted something between her and Chad that wasn't there. What had happened had to stop before it got further out of hand.

Out on the interstate, Chad drove in the steady stream of traffic headed south. "Izzy, are you ever going to look or speak to me again?"

Her heart thumped. She didn't want to have this discussion. She filled her voice with innocence. "I don't know what you mean."

"You know exactly what I'm talking about."

She looked back at the napping Henry. Anything not to have this discussion.

"The last thing you are is stupid." Chad's tone remained smooth and reassuring.

"Do we have to talk about it?" she asked softly but with a bite to the words.

"Apparently we do."

That got her attention. It wasn't like Chad

to use that tone with her except at work during an intense case.

"You need to let me know what you're thinking." He stopped at a light and his look bore into her despite his eyes being behind sunglasses.

She huffed. "Look, I embarrassed myself. And you last night. I appreciate you being a gentleman. That's all. Now it's been said."

"You might think so, but I think you're imagining something that's just not true."

Izzy turned to face him. Anger filled her. She recognized rejection. Knew it intimately. "Oh, no. I think I have a good handle on the situation."

"And I think you don't." His voice had turned tight. "I believe you're under the impression that I don't want you." He paused. "That's the furthest thing from the truth."

Some of the ice around her heart melted.

"In fact, I don't think I've ever wanted somebody more. What I don't want is you using me to get back at your ex. Or using me as your way to forget your ex. He still clouds your world far too much."

The air in the SUV hung thick with the weight of what Chad had just said. She saw the intensity of his feelings by the lift of his chin and the tightness of his jaw.

"Now that we've settled that. I want you to look at me and talk to me. Tell me something you'd like to do someday. Anything."

For the first time that morning, Izzy truly smiled. "You're a strange man, Chad McCain."

He grinned. "You're not the first person who has said that. I want to know. What would you like to do more than anything in the world? Someplace you'd like to go. Something you'd like to learn."

She didn't have to think about it. "I'd like to visit all the state capitals in the United States."

He looked at her long enough that Izzy said, "The road."

Chad's attention returned to his driving. "Sorry. I just hadn't expected that answer. Have you ever been to the capital in Atlanta?"

"Nope. It's on my list for my next day off."

"Then I'd like to be the one to show it to you." He glanced at her, wearing a smile.

"All right." Izzy returned his grin. "I answered your question. Now it's your turn. What would you like to do?"

His attention never left the road. "I have a long list of wants but right now most of all I'd like to kiss you again."

At that idea, heat flowed through Izzy and her smile grew larger.

* * *

Two days later Izzy passed Chad in the hallway of the ER unit. The notes of "Penny Lane" never failed to come across his lips. Izzy grinned. That tingly feeling he always created in her appeared. She shouldn't be so giddy about the personal attention he showed her, but she couldn't help but like it.

They hadn't seen each other except at work since their trip to Nashville. It was just as well. She needed some distance from him. Needed time to sort her feelings. Izzy wasn't sure there would ever be enough time for her to figure those out. She went between accepting the feelings that were growing in her and convincing herself she should stay as far away from him as possible. The problem was she lived in his backyard and worked with him. That wouldn't be easy.

Recently her saving grace had been they were on different shifts until today. Even now the ER had been so busy they hadn't had a chance to talk to each other. She'd deny it if asked but she missed him.

Izzy walked up to the unit desk. The unit tech said, "Dr. McCain has a fall patient coming into trauma one. You want to help him out?"

She couldn't say no. They made a great team in an emergency. "I'm on my way."

Izzy entered the room. The patient had just arrived. The EMTs were still giving Chad the report.

The girl had a four-by-four bandage lying over the right side of her forehead.

"Hi, I'm Izzy, one of the nurses. What's your name?"

"Judy."

"Judy, may I take a look at your injury?" Izzy smiled.

The girl nodded.

A two-inch laceration marred her young face. A red line of dried blood went over her eye and down her cheek.

"Can you tell me what happened?" Izzy asked.

Chad joined them then.

"I hit the street curb hard," the girl said.

Izzy said, "This is Dr. McCain. He's going to take care of you. He's nice and you'll like him."

Chad's look met hers for a second. His eyes twinkled.

"Judy, can you tell me what happened?"

"I was walking along. I just fell." She sounded perplexed.

Izzy looked to Chad. "I'll get her vitals."

Chad said to Judy, "I'm going to need to check your eyes. I'm afraid you might have a concussion." He pulled down on her bottom eyelid.

"I don't want to be here," Judy groaned.

Izzy spoke close to her ear. "I hate to say it but I'm afraid you're gonna have to stay. You need stitches and you need to be watched for a while. You took a hard hit to the head."

Chad spoke to Judy. "Can you follow my finger?" He moved his finger back and forth in front of her face. "What made you fall?"

"I don't know," the girl muttered.

"She just went down." A man who stood in the corner responded, adding, "I'm Judy's dad."

Chad asked Judy, "Does anything hurt? Other than your head."

"It was hurting before I fell."

Izzy's gaze met Chad's. That didn't sound good.

He nodded. Chad asked his next question in an unemotional voice, but Izzy recognized a note of concern. "Can you show me where?"

The girl pointed to the top right side of her head.

"Judy, I'm afraid you're going to have to join us here at hotel Atlanta Children's. You need to have some more tests run. I can promise you all the Jell-O you want and a visit to see an amazing fish aquarium. But before you have a chance at those amazing things, I'm going to need to put in some very eye-catching stitches in your head."

The girl gave Chad a half smile.

"It's that bad?" the father asked.

Chad nodded. "I suspect there's more going on than needing stitches. Izzy, I'm going to need a suture kit."

Izzy pulled a rolling tray over next to the bed with the kit already on it. She removed the bandage, then cleaned and sterilized the area around the laceration while Chad pulled on a gown and gloves.

"Judy, I'm not going to lie to you. This is going to hurt but soon it won't. Just hang in there with me. Izzy is going to hold your head steady. I need you to be very still. Dad, if you want, you can come hold her hand."

The father stepped to the other side of the bed and took Judy's hand.

"Are we all good?" He checked the group for nods. "Now, Judy, remember you can't move. Dad, why don't you tell us all about Judy's first Christmas?"

Chad was doing a good job of distracting the girl while he used a needle to numb the area around the wound. "It's going to take a few minutes for that medicine to work. While that's happening, Izzy and I are going to step out and find you a nice room for the night. We won't be gone long."

Izzy followed him out. Chad turned to her as soon as they were out in the hall with the door closed between them and the patient. "Will you call admissions and get her a room. I'm going to call neurology and get them on this case right away. One of her eyes is dilated. My best guess is a tumor."

"I'm on it."

"You always are." Chad smiled.

Ten minutes later they were back in the room stitching Judy's head. Izzy applied a bandage over the area.

"You're all done here. I understand they're blowing up the balloons and pulling out the party hats on the third floor to welcome you."

"No, they are not," Judy said with a dry tone and a hint of a smile.

Chad smiled. "You never know."

"Thanks, Doctor," Judy's father said.

"Not a problem." Chad looked at Judy. "I'll be checking on you. A tech will take you upstairs."

Izzy cleaned up the area while Chad moved on to his next case. Just when she thought he had been at his best, he went and moved the bar higher. He was wonderful with a girl who had to have been terrified. Chad made it hard for Izzy to stick to her plans to stay away from him.

Later that evening Chad leaned against the door facing Izzy's office as if he didn't have a care in the world. He was so handsome and wearing her favorite grin. Izzy's heart quivered. "Can I help you, Doctor?"

His cheeky grin turned wolfish. "Yes, you can. But I don't think you'll agree to it."

Heat built inside her, settling in her chest. He might be surprised. "Why're you hanging around at my door then?"

"I was going up to check on Judy and wondered if you'd like to go along?"

"I would like that. Thanks for asking." She closed the laptop she'd been working on.

They had started toward the elevators when Chad said, "I need to stop by the gift shop for a sec before we go up."

"Okay." She hadn't known him to frequent the store.

Five minutes later they were in the elevator going up. Chad held a large helium balloon in bright colors.

Izzy looked at him and smiled. Few people

would have thought to do something so nice for a child he really didn't know. "You're a special man, Dr. McCain."

"Thank you. Coming from you, that's high praise."

They walked to the third-floor desk and stopped. There all the female staff looked at Chad and smiled as if he might be their choice piece of candy.

"I'm Dr. McCain from the ER. Will you tell me what room Judy Reynolds is in?"

"Three twelve," a women said.

Walking toward the room and away from the desk, Izzy said in a low voice, "Well, you made an impression."

"How's that?" He sounded innocent as if he had no idea what she was talking about.

She looked at him with disbelief. "You didn't notice how all those women acted at seeing you holding a balloon. All their mouths dropped open, and they started to drool."

His gaze met hers, a grin on his lips. "Nope, I didn't notice. Did you drool too?"

Thankfully she didn't have to answer that because they had arrived at Judy's room. Chad knocked and pushed open the door. Judy lay in the bed, watching TV.

"Since you didn't believe me about the party, I thought Izzy and I would bring it to you."

The girl gave them both a genuine smile. She took the balloon from Chad.

Izzy suspected it but now it had been confirmed. Chad could charm the young and the old. She wasn't the only one who'd fallen under his spell. She might have been fighting tooth and nail not to have feelings for him but the man had a way about him. She couldn't keep pretending differently. Would it be so bad to explore what there was between them? Just see what happened?

They visited with Judy for a few minutes, then started back to the elevator.

"Henry's going to his grandparents' in the morning and will be gone until Sunday afternoon. Dr. Ricks gave me two tickets to see the Braves play tomorrow evening. I was wondering if you'd like to go?"

Izzy pursed her lips. She should say no but she didn't want to. "I don't know…" She paused. "But I do want to go. I love professional baseball. However, I have to work tomorrow until three. Will that be a problem?"

"Shouldn't be. The game starts at seven. We'll have plenty of time to get there."

Chad followed her back to her office. He stepped inside and closed the door.

"You need something else?" Izzy turned to him.

"I do. It's been too long." His arm reached around her waist, bringing her closer.

Izzy didn't have the willpower to stop him. She needed his kiss too.

Chad's lips found hers with a tender touch that was both stimulating and brief. He let her go and stepped back. "Sadly, again not the place or the time. But soon." He kissed her hard and fast. "Very soon."

He stepped to the door.

"Chad."

"Yeah?"

"I drooled too."

He grinned as he headed out the door. "Penny Lane" drifted back to her.

As determined as Chad was to keep his emotions in check where Izzy was concerned, he couldn't seem to resist her. It had become impossible for him to not think about her. He spent his nights arguing with himself over what was right for him, her and Henry. But the answers conflicted with his desires. She was a great nurse, a wonderful person, loving with Henry and made him want to kiss her senseless every time he saw her. The woman had him twisted up in a knot. One that he couldn't undo.

A prickle went through him when he took her hand while they walked to the baseball stadium, and she didn't resist. He craved her touch, enjoyed holding her hand. The problem was the more he was around Izzy, the more difficult it became to act unaffected by her.

"Are you really into baseball?" He knew few women who would have been as eager as her to go to a baseball game.

"I have been all my life." Her face alighted with pleasure as she looked around.

"You don't think it's kind of a slow game?" He guided her toward their entrance gate.

"Not for me. I like all of the tactical stuff. Which ball to throw. What goes into the coaching. There's nothing better than bases being loaded, a man up to bat with two outs and three balls count. You can't beat the drama. Anticipation. Then with a crack of the bat, he hits a home run."

Chad chuckled. "Yeah, you really are into it. So how do you feel about a stadium hot dog?"

She smiled. "Nothing better in the world."

"Then I guess that's what we'll be having. Unless you want to wait until we get home."

"A hot dog sounds perfect to me." Izzy beamed.

The desire to take her behind the stadium and kiss her almost got the better of him.

"It's not the only thing that's perfect."

Izzy's gaze met his. Chad's attention focused on her mouth. Unable to go without any longer, he kissed her. She leaned into him. The call of someone broke them apart. She looked shy and rattled. So sweet he wanted to kiss her again. "Come on. We don't want to miss the first throw."

As they continued toward the ballpark, a crowd gathered around them. They entered the stadium and found their seats.

"Wow, these are great seats. I'm impressed," Izzy said as they found their places five rows behind the Braves' dugout. "I'm going to be spoiled for my next game."

"You should be spoiled often but I can't take credit for the seats. Remember I was given the tickets."

"Still, you asked me to come along." She gave him a long meaningful look.

He cleared his throat. "I'll go get our food and be right back."

The national anthem had been sung and the first ball thrown out by the time he returned.

Chad grinned as he handed her the food. "You do know that you can sit back and still see."

"Yeah, but I like to be as close to the field as I can be." She took her drink and slipped it into the holder. "This is a truly amazing place and experience. Thank you for giving this to me."

"You're welcome." Chad settled in his seat and propped his foot up on the empty seat in front of him. Izzy looked cute dressed in blue jean shorts and a red T-shirt with a Braves logo on the sleeve. Her hair had been tucked up inside a ball cap.

With her food finished, Izzy moved back to the edge of her seat. He couldn't stop himself from running his hand across her back and could have sworn he heard her purring. Her focus remained on the field, but he sensed her awareness of his touch. He could keep it up for as long as she let him.

Hours later they walked out of the stadium hand in hand. This time Izzy had slipped hers into his. He smiled as if he were a kid who'd won a prize. They worked their way toward his car along with the mass of humanity.

As they walked in the early darkness, Izzy snuggled to him. "You must be cool." He wrapped an arm around her and pulled her close. At the SUV he ushered her into it.

"Thanks for today." She touched his arm. "I had a wonderful time."

"I noticed that. And I'm glad you did."

"A little intense, was I?"

"Just a little." He pulled out into the traffic. She giggled.

The sound rippled through him. There was something relaxing about Izzy's laugh. As if it could sooth any hurt. "Would you like to stop for something to eat?"

"I'm fine. I ate way too much at the game. If you want something, stop. I don't mind."

When had he rethought his stance on getting involved with Izzy? That's just it. He hadn't. She'd just happened. He'd thought he could resist her. With time he'd come to find out he couldn't. "I'm good too but I did have one more thing planned for the evening."

"What?"

Her eager look had him reconsidering it for going home and hopefully to his bed. With her. "I wanted to show you something. I think you would really like it. But it can wait until another time."

"No, let's do it now."

"Okay, if you really want to." He maneuvered the SUV out onto the interstate.

"I do."

He drove past the turn off to his house and continued downtown.

"Where're we going?" Izzy demanded.

Her curiosity was one of many things he liked about her. "Wait and see. I want it to be a surprise." Chad turned off onto a drive with few lights. He came out of the tree-lined street and pulled into a large empty parking lot.

"Oh, my goodness. It's beautiful." Awe filled Izzy's voice as she looked at the grand building with a bright gold dome glowing in the flood-lights. "Can we get out?"

"Sure."

They met each other at the front of the car. Chad leaned back against the grill, and she did the same beside him.

"I thought you might appreciate seeing the Georgia Capitol Building after dark. Or have you already seen it?"

"No, I haven't. I've only really gone between the hospital and home and back again." She grinned. "With the exception of trips to the grocery store."

He gave her a nudge with his shoulder. "You're not going to let me forget that, are you?"

"I doubt it." Her focus remained on the Capitol. "It's magnificent. Thank you for bringing me here."

"On our next day off, we'll tour the inside." Before Izzy, he would have never had an interest in doing so. He wanted to show her everything.

Her head went back so she could look at the tip-top of the dome. "What makes the gold paint glow so?"

"That's real gold. From Dahlonega, a small town in north Georgia. The gold was brought down here in wagons pulled by mules. The dome is gold leaf." He might sound like a history teacher but Izzy hung on every word. His ego grew.

"That's amazing," she said in admiration. "So beautiful."

He watched Izzy. Not unlike her.

"Thank you for showing me this." She kissed his cheek.

Heat shot through him. "I think you can do better than that."

Chad brought her around to stand between his spread legs as he continued to lean against the SUV. His mouth found hers. Izzy came up on her toes and met his kiss. His hands went to her waist and slipped under her T-shirt to find warm silky skin. She wiggled against him. His manhood shot to rock-hard. Her mouth opened. Chad entered, wanting to devour her.

He needed her gentle ways. Her steadfastness. The serenity she brought to those around her. The peace she somehow brought to his life. He needed to inhale it, surround himself in it, hold on to it.

He eased away from the kiss. "I think we should take this somewhere else."

CHAPTER SEVEN

HALF AN HOUR later Chad pulled into his driveway and stopped the SUV behind Izzy's car.

Their relationship had grown to something he didn't want to define. He should leave her alone, couldn't make promises about tomorrow. Yet there was something between them, something he'd never had with another woman. No matter how hard he pushed it away, the desire to explore it remained. As undefined as it was, there was still a rightness to it. They fit. For right now at least.

Not wanting to scare Izzy away, he had to be careful, but he also didn't want the evening to end. He had so few nights that were all to himself. Henry would return tomorrow. "Since there's a nice breeze, why don't we sit in the backyard for a while? I'll get us both a drink."

"That sounds nice. Why don't you let me get the drinks since my kitchen is closer? Would you like iced tea or water or something stronger?"

To his immense pleasure, she'd agreed. He hadn't been confident she would. "A cold beer?"

"I should be able to fill that order." She headed toward her door.

Chad settled into the metal chair. Leaning his head back, he closed his eyes. He listened as Izzy open and closed her door. A few minutes later, her soft steps came toward him. He knew the moment she stood in front of him without looking because the scent that was hers alone filled the air. He smiled. What a lovely smell. Chad opened his eyes.

"I thought you might have gone to sleep." She looked down on him.

"Nope. Just listening to the night sounds." And for her. He found Izzy as peaceful as a quiet night. He reached for the beer bottle she held, taking a long swallow as Izzy settled into the empty chair beside his.

"It's been a nice evening." Her words were so soft he almost missed them. "I had fun at the ball game. I loved seeing the Capitol. Thanks for sharing that with me."

Chad hadn't felt this content in a long time. He wished it could stay that way. Izzy made his busy, stressful single-parent life easier by just being around. He would worry about tomorrow then. Right now, all he wanted to do was pull Izzy into his lap and kiss her senseless. Then take her to bed and love her to the point she was too weak to get out of bed.

He inhaled deeply and released it slowly. What was happening to him? Izzy. He didn't say anything for a few minutes.

"What were you thinking?" Izzy asked.

Did he dare tell her? "Do you really want to know?"

She didn't immediately answer as if she knew her response would change everything between them. "Yeah, I do."

"I think there's something special between us. I'm not sure what it is or where it can go, but I know it's special enough that it would be a shame not to act on it." Izzy didn't say anything. His throat tightened. Had he misjudged the situation?

He glanced at Izzy. She smiled. Even in the darkness, he could tell. "I'd be lying to you if I didn't tell you I'd like to have you in my bed."

Her intake of breath had him watching her. He took another gulp of his drink. When she stood, his heart sank. She was going in and leaving him to wallow in his need.

"Mine's closer."

Heat shot through him. "Are you saying what I hope you're saying?"

Izzy offered him her hand. "For a very intelligent man, you can be awful slow sometimes."

He put his bottle on the ground, got to his feet and took her hand. She led him to her door. Opening it, she stepped inside. He followed.

She turned. Her hands went to his chest, traveled up to his shoulders, across them, then returned to wrap around his neck. She nipped at his bottom lip, then pressed her lush mouth on his. With her chest against his, she kissed him deeply. His already-thick manhood twitched. His hands trembled as they cupped her butt and brought her against him.

"Not that I'm complaining but what made you agree?"

"I trust you. You make me feel special. Make love to me, Chad."

"Sweetheart, I promise you can always trust me, and you are unique." He would show Izzy just how special he thought she was. "Izzy, you need to know that I'm not looking for anything permanent. All I can offer is tonight."

"That's enough. I'm good with just tonight. I just needed to feel wanted."

"You are wanted, have no doubt of that."

Izzy moved toward the bed. He reached for her pulling her back to him. He brought her into the circle of his arms and tenderly kissed her. She melted into him. His manhood throbbed. Izzy opened for him when he teased the seam of her lips. She deepened the kiss as if she needed reassurance of her desirability. He intended to show her she was that and so much more.

What he wouldn't do was pounce on her like a starving man.

Chad brushed his fingers along her arms until his tangled with hers. He continued to give her gentle kisses along her neck. Izzy made little noises of pleasure that fed his desire. His hands moved to her waist, where he slowly gathered her T-shirt in search of bare skin, making circles at her waist and back with his thumb.

Izzy purred in appreciation.

His manhood tightened. Chad reminded himself to go slow and easy. He hadn't expected Izzy's easy acceptance or aggressiveness. Not that he minded. In fact, it turned him on more. His marriage had been so lackluster in the sex department. He enjoyed having someone who acted excited about being with him.

This wasn't the practical and cautious Izzy. He suspected he was seeing the real Izzy, open wide and alive. His heart raced at the thought of experiencing that passion. Yet he wanted to savor her. He needed her to feel treasured.

"I think we need to slow this down a little. I'd like to make it last."

Her hands stilled. She stepped back, looking away.

This was the last thing he wanted. Using a curled finger, he lifted her chin until she met his gaze. "Hey, nobody's complaining here. To the contrary. Don't turn away from me now."

"I wondered if you thought I was coming on too strong. I've been accused of that before."

"Stop thinking such garbage. Whatever *he* said, he was wrong. On every level. As far as I'm concerned, you're perfect."

A genuine smile formed on her lips. "Thanks for thinking so. You're pretty perfect as well."

"Now where were we?" He lowered his head. "Somewhere right about here." His lips tenderly found hers as he lifted her T-shirt. Chad pulled it over her head, dropping it to the floor.

Izzy didn't move. She watched him as he cupped a breast. Full, ripe, he judged its weight before he brushed the pad of his thumb over the skin along the line of her bra. She felt warm and smooth beneath his finger. "So beautiful."

She trembled. Her heart raced beneath his hand. He couldn't remember ever being so well rewarded from a touch. Leaning down, he kissed the top curve of her breast where his thumb caressed. "I love how responsive you are."

Her hand slipped into his hair, holding him to her as his lips traveled over her skin, finding her nipple beneath her bra. The other hand pulled at his shirt until she touched the skin of his back. Her fingers kneaded his muscles, encouraging his attention. He pushed at her bra until both her breasts were visible.

Lifting one, Chad placed a kiss on the tip of her nipple. "So beautiful." His gaze captured her dazed one. "May I see how delicious it tastes?"

Izzy mouth parted slightly but no sound came out. Her eyes filled with the foggy look of delight and anticipation. Her breath hitched as his mouth surrounded her nipple. He tugged, then circled it with his tongue. Izzy moaned. Her hands on each side of his head held him to her. With a flick of his fingers, he released the back clasp of her bra and removed it, letting it go the way of her shirt. As he did, Izzy pushed at his shirt. He jerked it off. The cloth floated to the floor.

When he would have brought her against him, she held him away with her palms against his chest. "It's my turn to admire you."

* * *

Izzy had promised herself she wouldn't step off into deep water where Chad was concerned. That had changed quickly. She found him impossible to avoid. It looked as if she needed a rowboat if her heart was to survive the onslaught of Chad's lovemaking. Her mind had stopped working. All she could do was feel. Chad's desire for her showed in his every touch. It empowered her. She'd felt weak for so long.

Chad stood, his hands featherlight as they glided up and down her arms while she explored his chest. She ran her fingers through the dusting of hair in the center. Teased his nipples with her teeth before she kissed them. All the time her hands were moving across his skin. She marveled at the flex and pull of the muscles beneath their warm covering. Everything about Chad felt right. Strong, steady and secure. She was safe with him.

She heard the hiss of his breath when her distended nipples brushed his chest. She went up on her toes to kiss his chin. He was as sensitive to her touch as she was to his. Her lips traveled along his jaw as her hands worked the button of his khaki shorts.

"I think it's time I got involved here." Chad's words were a low growl that rumbled through her. His mouth covered hers in a hot wet kiss as he crushed her tightly against him.

She wanted more and more of Chad. Her hands returned to the clasp of his shorts. She found the zipper. Below it lay his length, thick and hard, waiting for her. Her center had gone wet in anticipation. This need growing in her hungered for appeasement. By this man.

Chad's mouth remained on hers as his hands came to her waist, then up to tease the outer curves of her breasts.

She returned his kisses while she slowly lowered his zipper. Her fingers brushed his length with the back of her hand. She wished his underwear were gone.

Chad's kiss gentled as she pushed his pants to the floor. When she would have gone after his underwear, his hand stopped her. "I think you have some catching up to do."

She pressed against him, appreciating the heat of his skin in the air-conditioned room. As his hands moved down her sides, goose bumps that had nothing to do with the temperature rose along her skin.

Chad led her to the bed. He sat and brought her between his legs, facing him. She rested her hands on his shoulders.

"I want to see all of you." His hands traveled to the waistband of her shorts. He worked the button open and the zipper. With hands on her hips, he tugged, letting the fabric drop to her feet.

Izzy toed off her tennis shoes and stepped out of her shorts.

Chad wasted no time in sending her panties to the floor. She stood bare and exposed in front of him. Chad inhaled sharply.

He held her at arm's length. Izzy watched as he studied her. She moved to cover herself, but his hand circled her wrist and held it. "Izzy, you're amazing. Breathtaking. Magnificent."

Each adjective made her heart swell. Izzy's body grew hotter.

"Come here. I want to touch you." He brought her closer. His hand rested on one hip while the other brushed along her thigh, down to her knee, then up again to her hip.

She shivered, shaking with longing.

Chad's fingers went down to her knee again. He teased the hollow place in the back. He used her inner thigh as the pathway up. Her body reacted as if it were an instrument humming to only a tune Chad could play. Her center tingled in anticipation of his touch, drummed with need. Instead of giving her relief, his fingers moved to her other thigh. Again, going to her knee. That patience and thoroughness he was known for in the ER might drive her crazy.

Izzy's fingers bit into his shoulders. Her body swamped with aching need, making it difficult to stand.

Chad's gaze captured hers as his touch moved upward again. "Tell me what you want, Izzy. Let me give it to you."

"Touch me." The words were a soft beg.

He brushed her curls. Her legs widened. She wanted more. His finger ran across her heated center. Her knees wobbled.

"Steady." Chad's hand tightened on her hip. "I'm just getting started with loving you."

Izzy wasn't sure she could stand much more.

His damp finger ran along her thigh but soon returned to the arch of her legs. This time he found her center and entered.

Izzy whimpered. Chad pulled his finger away and returned. His mouth found her breast. He mimicked with his tongue what he did with his finger. Izzy held onto him for dear life as her body twitched and jerked while her center tightened and curled in on itself. She pushed down on Chad's hand, asking, then grasping, for that supreme relief. It came as a blast of pleasure that made her throw back her head, close her eyes and moan. Her entire body shook and sank against Chad.

He lifted her to the bed. Looking down on her, he smiled. "Heavens, you're beautiful."

With her eyes still glazed with bliss, her body sedated, she said, "I can assure you that you may take all the credit for it."

Chad chuckled. "You do know how to build a man's ego."

She cupped his cheek. "And you know how to give a woman an experience of a lifetime."

A wicked look formed on his face as his eyes gleamed. "I'm not done yet."

Izzy sighed. "I sure hope not."

Chad stood and removed his underwear. Finding his shorts, he took out his wallet and pulled a condom from it.

Izzy watched his movements with fascination. "I can appreciate a prepared doctor."

"More like a hopeful one." He started to open the package.

Izzy curled a finger and called him forward. "Come here first. Let me admire you."

He hesitated a moment. "I don't know if I can stand much admiration at this point."

"Let's just see." She offered him her best pleading look while moving to sit on the side of the bed.

Chad stepped to her. Izzy's hand circled his aching manhood. His breath hissed on its way in. Her hand stroked him. His jaw tightened. This couldn't go on much longer. She met his gaze as she pumped her hand as far down as possible and back again.

"That's it." He growled and removed Izzy's hand. Taking the foil package, he said, "Move to the center of the bed." Seconds later he was covered and joined her. His lips found hers as he positioned himself between her legs. She wrapped them around his waist pulled him to her. Unable to wait any longer, he entered Izzy.

She took all of him, nudging him closer with her heels. Encouraging him. Her arms came around his neck, and she clung as he pumped into her. She was everything he'd dreamed of at night and imagined during the day. Warm, welcoming and responsive.

Too quickly he climbed the peak. Seconds later Izzy pulled her mouth from his, stiffened and eased as a soft sigh of her release whispered by his ear. He made one final plunge and exploded into oblivion that could only be described as extraordinary.

He was in trouble. If he only had one night with Izzy, he better make the most of it.

When he could catch his breath, he rolled to her, gathering her to him, and kissed her temple. "Izzy, I don't know what to say but thank you."

"Mmm…"

Her eyes were closed. She slept. Standing on shaky knees, he moved the covers back and placed her under them. He then climbed in beside her, pulling her against his chest. She snuggled in close. This was what made a perfect moment. He listened to her gentle breathing for a few minutes before he joined her in rest.

Sunlight was just beginning to show through the large picture window the next morning as Chad came out of the bathroom to find Izzy still sprawled naked on her stomach in the bed. She reminded him of a golden goddess in a Renaissance painting. His manhood instantly hardened. He wanted her again. In the most basic way. To mark her as his. Standing at the edge of the bed, he grabbed her ankles and pulled her toward him.

"Huh?" She looked back with hooded eyes.

His hands ran up her legs to her waist. He pulled her hips up to him. When she would have turned, he kissed her shoulder. "Stay on your knees."

She stilled.

His finger found her center and teased until she was ready. His other hand fondled a breast. Izzy wiggled her butt against his thick length, almost sending him over the edge.

He groaned. His manhood throbbed. "I can't wait any longer." Seconds later, after grabbing a condom, he pressed into her.

Izzy moaned. She raised her hips, giving him better access. He thrust into her. She took him without complaint. The pleasure of having her was almost more than his control would allow.

"Join me, Izzy."

She raised her hips higher. Her body shuttered. She drew his name out as her orgasm washed over her. Moments later his body shook with the force of his release, one that blinded him to nothing else but the sweetness of Izzy.

She lay on her stomach, panting. He fell half on her and half on the bed. He kissed her shoulder blade as his hand ran along her waist and over the rise of her behind. "Sweetheart, that was amazing. I'm sorry I took you like a barbarian. When I saw your sweet bottom, I had to have you."

Izzy rolled to face him. "I'm not complaining." She kissed him. "Now, hush so I can get some sleep so we can do it again."

A chuckle rippled through him. "Sounds like a plan."

His arm lay over her waist. What was to become of them? After last night he didn't know if he could give up Izzy. She would never accept half measures and he couldn't offer her more. She wanted marriage and children. He'd been down that road before. He didn't know if he could do it again, even to keep Izzy.

She shifted and snuggled into him. Her hair smelled of flowers as it tickled his chin. His chest had a knot in it. The more painful question would be how could he ever let her go?

Izzy woke to a warm male next to her. It took her a few moments to realize where she was and who was with her. A Mona Lisa smile crept to her lips. She had a secret. It was Chad McCain. Right now he was all hers.

She hated to leave him and his warmth, but hadn't they agreed this would be temporary? She shouldn't get used to having him close. She made a trip to the bathroom. Chad still slept. Izzy resisted the temptation to slide back into bed. Instead she went to the kitchen. He would be hungry when he woke.

Quietly she prepared omelets and toast. It was almost time to call him for breakfast when she heard the low rumble of, "Good morning."

Chad sat on the edge of the bed with his chest bare and a sheet across his hips. His tussled hair and morning stubble covering his chin gave him a sexy look.

Maybe she should forget about breakfast

until later. The grumble of Chad's belly ended that idea. He stood and she turned away. She couldn't take anymore. The man spoke to her on a physical level as well as an emotional one. For however long it lasted, she intended to enjoy it. She'd figure out the rest later.

Chad pulled on his jeans not bothering to button them. What was his plan? Torture her?

She returned her attention to the omelet. Chad reached around her and moved the pan off the heat. He kissed the back of her neck, then turned her to face him. "Every morning should start with breakfast and a little sugar. Not necessarily in that order."

His lips found hers. Izzy's arms, with a spatula still in one hand, went around his neck. She leaned into him, accepting all he'd give. This she would take for as long as she could get it. However short that might be.

The sound of his stomach complaining again broke them apart.

"I think I better get some food into you."

He grinned, then gave her a quick kiss on the cheek. "I'm going to the bathroom, and I'll be right back."

He was as good as his word and soon returned. Izzy had their places set on the bar. Their food waited.

"This smells good and looks wonderful. You

could spoil me with your cooking." Chad dug in with gusto.

He could spoil her by just being there. Izzy spent most of her meal watching Chad. He looked perfectly at home here with her. She studied the way his shoulder muscles moved as he forked food into his mouth. Last night she'd enjoyed every ridge and dip to her heart's content.

His look met hers with a raised brow. "You're not eating."

"No."

"You better eat. I have some physical activity planned for you today." His look of desire made her middle flutter with want.

"I thought we only had last night." Izzy needed to slow herself down.

His lips turned teasing. "I thought we might extend it until this afternoon unless you have an objection."

She bit into her toast. "What do you have planned?"

Chad's gaze caught and held hers, his eyes having taken on a predatory look. "I want to take you back to bed and make slow love to you. Then I'm going to take you downtown to a nice hotel for lunch. I don't have to pick up Henry until four, so I think I'll bring you back here and love you a little more."

Izzy put her finger on her bottom lip and tapped. "It sounds doable."

"So you don't have a problem with my plans?" Heat flickered in his eyes.

Warmth streamed through her, pooling at her center. "Not at all."

The next few days Izzy lived in a cloud of blissful memories and sadness. Thoughts of her and Chad's time together heated her while at the same time disappointment cooled her, knowing they wouldn't be together again. Unfortunately it was the way it must be. That's what they had agreed to.

In such a brief time, Chad had captured her heart. She'd tried and failed not to let him and Henry draw her in. Staying emotionally uninvolved had been impossible. Especially after the passionate lovemaking Chad and she had shared over the weekend.

He'd said nothing about his feelings or wanting anything more before he left to pick up Henry. Instead he'd given her a long hot kiss that curled her toes.

The worst thing was having to see Chad at the hospital. She had to force herself not to react when his hand accidently brushed hers. Or let it show when her hands trembled if he stepped too close. Still, she couldn't help but grin like a silly schoolgirl when she heard the notes of "Penny Lane" when he walked by her or passed her office.

It did help they were on opposite schedules, but it hurt as well. On the days she wasn't working, she eagerly waited for the sound of the SUV pulling up the drive. With great restraint she kept from going to him. She refused to let on how much she wanted him back in her bed. Somehow she had to put a stop to this needed that gnawed at her.

They had agreed to keep what had happened between them just that—between them. She feared she wasn't that good of an actress, but she gave it her best effort. Even Ms. Weber, who Izzy was beginning to call a true friend, gave her a speculative look when Chad was mentioned.

On the Thursday evening after their weekend, there was a knock at her apartment door. She looked up from the book she'd been trying to read.

"Hey, can I come in?" Chad asked from outside the screen door.

Izzy stood, cramming her hands into the back pockets of her jean shorts. "Sure."

"How are you doing?"

"I'm fine." Great. They were back to acting like strangers.

"Uh, about this past weekend. I haven't had a chance to say how much I enjoyed spending time with you. I should have said that before now."

Was he feeling as unsure around her as she was around him? "I thought it was nice also."

"So we're still good?"

"Yeah, we're good."

He shifted on his feet for a moment. "I noticed you have the day off tomorrow, and I don't have to be in until seven for the evening shift. I promised to take you to the Capitol. I like to keep my promises. If you want to go, I'll see if Ms. Weber will come a little earlier to watch Henry."

For her own sake, she should decline but she didn't want to. The problem was she loved doing anything if she was with Chad. How easily she'd fallen back into the pattern she'd had with Richard. Making her world revolve around a man. But Chad wasn't just any man. "I'd like to go."

"Then I'll check with Ms. Weber. We'll do tourist things for a while. Maybe sneak a kiss or two in a dark corner." He winked.

Izzy's blood zipped. She had no idea how much she'd missed a man flirting with her. Chad did it so well. "We'll see."

"Okay. I understand. I like spending time with you, and I'll accept that."

Izzy smiled, one she meant. "Good because your friendship is important to me."

"I feel the same." He returned her smile.

The next day Chad found a parking place close to the Capitol and they entered through a side entrance. Soon they stood in the rotunda looking up at the beautiful artwork.

"This is truly amazing," Izzy said in awe.

She glanced at Chad to find him watching her. Her cheeks turned warm. "I must sound like a silly girl."

"Not at all. I'm glad you're enjoying yourself."

He sounded as if it was important to him that she was happy. "Isn't this where they stand on the steps when giving a press conference?" She pointed to the large marble stairs in the center of the Capitol building.

"Yep. At least I know you keep up with the local news. Come this way. I want to show you what a fifth-grade boy liked most when he visited the Capitol a long time ago." He took her hand.

With a feeling of rightness, she let him.

"I hope it's still here."

They went around a couple of corners.

"There it is." Chad proudly put out a hand.

"Ooh." She squished up her nose. "It's a two-headed calf."

A sheepish look came over Chad's face. "I guess it's wasted on a girl."

She gave him a teasing slap on his arm. "You do need to work on you dating skills."

His eyes took on a wicked look. "I don't have to when I have other skills."

Izzy flushed. On that they could agree.

He studied her a moment. "Hungry? I know a burger dive a couple of blocks from here."

"Sounds good. It won't have any two-headed animals, will it?"

Chad chuckled. "Nope. They'd already be hamburger anyway."

They walked toward the exit door.

Izzy stopped to look through the window of the senate meeting room. "Thanks for bringing me here. It's very impressive."

As they continued down the marble hallway, they passed three men, one walking ahead of the others. The one in front smiled and said, "Hello."

Chad answered, "Hello, Governor."

When they were outside, Izzy turned to Chad. "Was that really the governor?"

"Yes." Chad wore a huge grin.

"You spoke to the governor." She looked back at the door in amazement.

Chad chuckled and led her toward the SUV. "Come on. Let's go eat."

They entered the diner that look like it belonged in the 1950s, complete with metal tables and chairs with red plastic seats. Chad settled her at a table. A few minutes later the waiter took their order. Soon their burger plates were place in front of them.

"This place is something." Izzy wrestled with her lettuce, tomato and onion that continued to slip out from the bun.

Chad grinned. "I can tell you're enjoying it. You've got ketchup on the tip of your nose."

Izzy giggled.

"Don't do that." Chad's voice turned tight.

"You don't like my laugh?" Hurt filled her chest. She looked at Chad, finding him watching her with a flame of want in his eyes.

His heated gaze remained on her. "The problem is I like it too much. If you don't want to miss out on that burger because I've taken you out to the car and had my way with you, I'd be careful."

"Chad, we agreed to one night. I can't keep my distance if you talk like that."

"Izzy, I can't promise you tomorrow, or all the things you want. But I can promise we can have a good time together. Enjoy each other's company. Do things together. We're good together. Great in fact. I don't want to give that up and I hope you don't either." He looked deep into her eyes. "I ache for you. One night isn't going to be enough for me."

At least Chad was being upfront where Richard hadn't been. Chad wasn't making promises he couldn't or wouldn't keep. He wasn't planning to use her. She ached for him too. More than she ever dreamed she could. She'd go into this relationship with her eyes open. "Then we can agree to a fling?"

"As long as if works for both of us." A wolfish gleam came to his eyes. "Henry and Ms. Weber should be napping by the time we get home. Maybe we could put that time to good use."

She smiled. "I'd like that. A lot."

Saturday a week later Chad knocked on Izzy's door. She greeted him dressed in a large T-shirt that just hit the top of her thighs and a smile. He swallowed hard. "I hope you don't open the door dressed like that for everyone."

"No, I save this outfit for special people."

He grinned. What had he done to deserve being this happy? The only thing that would have improved the moment was if it had taken place in his bed when he woke that morning. It was killing him to keep Izzy at a distance when he only wanted to have her next to him. His attraction to Izzy he'd fought from the beginning. Even at the grocery store before he'd even known her, there had been something. She made his emotions whirl. He was waiting on his brain to catch up.

The last week had been nice. She'd shared a few meals with him and Henry. Had stayed after to watch some TV. He'd not realized how lonely he had become. It was nice to have someone around. It was especially nice to have Izzy close. To share a laugh. Sneak a kiss. Have someone whom he looked forward to seeing at the end of the day.

Like now he couldn't resist pulling her to him and giving her a quick kiss on the lips. "Henry wants to go to the zoo. Would you like to go with us?"

"That sounds like fun."

Chad remained in the doorway, afraid if he went inside it might be a while before he came out. If only Henry could be left alone… It had been days since they'd had sex. Instead of physical activity, Chad had made a point to make Izzy feel wanted out of bed by spending time talking to her while they watched Henry play, or by inviting her to dinner at his house or just small touches. "We'll go to Piedmont Park afterward for a picnic."

She pushed her hair back out of her eyes. "Sounds good to me. Do I need to fix anything?"

"Nope. Henry and I'll take care of everything. Today you just get to enjoy." He pulled her to him again. This time he allowed her to return his kiss. "See you in twenty minutes."

With a lightened step Chad strolled to the house, looking forward to spending the day with his two favorite people. That feeling he could only describe as euphoric. It had been so long since he'd felt that way it took him a moment to recognize it for what it was. He hummed "Penny Lane" as he entered the house.

Yet something niggled at the back of his mind. How long could things stay the way they were before he or she wanted more? Or less? He'd long ago decided he wasn't husband material and that's want Izzy wanted. Chad winced. How could he ever let her walk away?

They were in the SUV on the way to the Zoo Atlanta when Izzy asked Henry, "What's your favorite animal?"

"Lions."

"Do you think you'll see one today?"

Henry nodded.

"What's your favorite?" Chad asked her.

"I like the giraffes." She looked a Henry. "They have those long necks."

"How about you?" Izzy touched Chad's arm.

"I'm a polar bear guy." A few minutes later, he pulled into the parking lot of the zoo. There he strapped Henry into his stroller. "Let's go see if we can find all our favorite animals."

As they walked toward the entrance, Izzy said, "I'm impressed with how you handled that stroller."

At her approval, his chest expanded. "I can't say it didn't take time to learn."

"Most things worth learning do. You're a good father, Chad. The way you treat Henry, your patients and me, I think you must have been a better husband than you give yourself credit for. You have nothing to feel guilty about."

"Thanks. Coming from you that means a lot."

She stopped, gave him a long look, then a smile. One of those that he felt in his chest. "I meant it."

"Go, Daddy." Henry wiggled all over, shaking the stroller. "See lions."

Chad and Izzy laughed, then Chad said, "Let's go see some lions."

They found the lions first. Henry and Izzy

spent a long time talking about what they were doing and what they ate. Chad enjoyed the interaction between the two. The excitement on their faces was infectious. Izzy would make a wonderful mother. And wife.

For some reason that didn't strike fear in his heart. His mind was going places he had closed off. Could he or Henry stand it emotionally to open that door? Was he ready to make that step?

They stopped to see the polar bears as they worked their way around the zoo. When they came to the snake habitat, Izzy said, "I believe I'll just wait out here."

"You sure you don't want to go in?" Chad teased.

She pursed her lips in the cutest way. "I'll be fine right here."

Chad whispered in her ear, brushing his lips across her cheek. "And I thought you were fearless."

He and Henry went inside the dark room. When they returned, Izzy waited for them in the bright sunlight. Ironically that's how he thought of her. As a shining light in his life. Chad shook his head. He had it bad. If he weren't careful, he'd break out in song. Seconds later he caught himself humming "Penny Lane."

"I've been looking at the map. It looks like the giraffes are just around the next turn," Izzy said.

"Giraffes," Henry squeaked.

Chad raised his brow at her.

She grinned. "It's just as important to know when you can scream as it is to know when to be quiet."

Chad leaned close, making sure no one else could hear. "I like it when you scream."

Izzy's eye twinkled as her cheeks pinked.

He watched with a feeling of rightness settling in his chest as Izzy and Henry enjoyed talking about the giraffes. Henry was fearful at first but soon warmed up to the large animals with Izzy's encouragement.

From there they started making their way back to the car. Ahead of them was a family of five. One child was in a stroller and the other two held the hands of a parent. At one time he'd wanted that. Maybe it wouldn't be so horrible to want that again. To have more babies. Brothers and sisters for Henry. A wife for him.

But could he be the right husband and father for them? He couldn't and wouldn't give up his medicine. He'd not been enough for Nan. What made him think he could be enough for someone else? Today he and Izzy and Henry were just playing family. What happened when life got hard?

He looked at Izzy. Still, she had his mind wandering places he'd once said he'd never travel again.

CHAPTER EIGHT

THREE DAYS LATER a staff member stood at her door. "Izzy, Chad asked for your help in trauma two. We have a go-cart accident patient."

Izzy hated that. They were the worst. Mangled children were tough cases. "Tell him I'm on my way."

Izzy closed the laptop, pulled her hair back in a band and headed out the door. When she arrived, the boy lay on the gurney with his eyes closed. Izzy had no doubt Chad had given him medicine to help him rest and relieve his pain.

Chad was already busy issuing orders. "I need X-rays, full routine lab work, vitals and IV antibiotics going. Use the uninjured arm for those. We need to cut the clothes off. Izzy, I need you with me. While I check for internal injuries can you start cleaning him up?" He looked up and down the bloody body of the eight-year-old boy. "We're going to need at least six suture kits to start. I'd like you to assist."

Izzy went to the storage cabinet and pulled out the kits, setting them on a movable tray. "I'm going next door to get two more. Anything else we need?"

"More saline and plenty of four-by-fours. This boy didn't win against the tree."

Izzy hurried to gather the supplies. When she returned, the X-ray techs were there. As soon as they finished, she and Chad moved in again along with the other staff to do their jobs.

"The plastic surgeon on call needs to be notified," Chad said to no one in particular.

"Done," a nurse called.

Izzy smiled. Her staff knew their jobs. "Sherry, help me clean up this boy so Dr. McCain can go to work."

Chad jerked off his plastic gloves. "I'm going out to talk to the parents a moment while you're getting him ready for stitches. They must be worried."

Izzy and the nurse went to work removing the blood from around the wounds. Chad quickly returned. He pulled on fresh plastic gloves. Izzy put on a fresh pair as well.

Chad's chin when to his chest. His eyes closed and he took a deep breath.

"Chad?" Izzy looked at him with concern.

His shadowed gaze met hers. He looked like his mind had gone somewhere else.

"You okay?"

"Yeah." His eyes cleared. "Let's do the laceration on his leg first. It looks like the deepest and longest. I suspect the X-ray is going to show that the left arm is broken. We'll wait on that one. The one on his shoulder we'll do next and work our way down to the smallest. When Plastic gets here, they'll handle those on his face."

Izzy popped the top on the saline bottle and poured it over the long wound. Had Chad been thinking about how Henry had looked after the accident?

"Watch for any debris." Chad adjusted the large light above them. He was back with her now. They leaned over until their heads were almost touching.

"There's something." Izzy pointed to a spot inside the wound.

Chad picked up long tweezers and pulled out a piece of bark. "Well done."

They continued to search as Izzy poured. Satisfied they had found everything, Chad opened a suture kit and went to work.

Izzy said to Sherry, "Start cleaning the other wounds while I help Chad."

He made small stitches inside the wound. She dabbed the gauze in the wound, making sure Chad could see. As he finished knotting each stitch, she cut the thread.

Izzy glanced up at Chad, whose look remained on the stitches he was placing in the boy's arm. He methodically went about his work. His hand remained steady as he made the hoops and twists.

For hours they worked, getting the boy's injuries closed. Izzy's shoulders ached. Just as they finished, a plastic surgeon walked into the room.

"Glad to see you, Pete." Chad removed his gloves and threw them in the trash. "The patient is all yours. You'll pass him off to Orth to set his arm."

"I hate to see these go-cart injuries. They sure can mess up a kid." The tall thin man wearing green scrubs studied the boy's face.

"I couldn't agree more." Chad turned to her. "Good work." He looked to Sherry. "Nice job." Chad rolled his shoulders.

Izzy wished she could massage them but that would be noticed and commented on.

He dropped the gown and mask in the garbage bin on the way out the door.

Minutes after she returned to her office, Chad entered without bothering to knock. He flopped into a chair and ran his hands over his face, then through his hair. "I hate those cases. It's almost more than I can do to get though them. Children mangled in accidents. The auto ones are always the worst, but go-carts are up there."

Izzy came around the desk, closing the door as she moved toward him. She stood close beside him. Chad reached around her waist, bringing her close. She returned his hug, pressing his head into her chest as she ran her fingers through his hair.

"I know they must be difficult with your history. But Henry is safe."

"It's just that I see him in every one of those cases. It drags up all those horrible memories. If I hadn't upset Nan, she might not have had the accident."

"You're just guessing that. You'll never know exactly what happened. You can't keep blaming yourself for everything."

"Easier said than done. You made it better today by being beside me. And now. Somehow you make it all easier." He gave her a gentle squeeze.

"That's nice to hear." Izzy looked at him, giving him a weak smile. "I'm here for you."

"I never doubted it."

"Good."

He looked at her. "You're strong, passionate, bighearted and dependable. I can count on you. You don't know how much that means to me."

She kissed him on the forehead. "It means a lot to me to hear you say that."

"I mean every word."

His phone rang. He answered. "I'm needed in the ER."

She gave him a quick kiss on the lips. "I'll tell you what, why don't you and Henry come to my place tonight for supper. We can all watch a movie together. Have a slow easy evening. Decompress."

He stood. "Thanks. I don't know what we did before you came into our lives."

That evening Chad entered Izzy's apartment to the smell of something hot and fresh. Home cooking. Better than that, Izzy stood at the stove. Her face flushed from the heat.

She came to him and took Henry, who received a big kiss. "Hello, handsome."

"Down." Henry wiggled. She put him down to go play with toys from a basket she kept for him near the sofa.

"Hey." Izzy looked at Chad when he stepped forward. Interest showed in her eyes. She gave him another look, this one from head to toe. Heat shot through him. "I like that look on you. A tight T-shirt and jeans. You're rocking the sexy doc look."

He walked up behind her, pushed her hair to the side and kissed her behind the ear.

"Mmm… I like you. So sweet."

"I like you too." Why did he feel better just being in Izzy's presence? She drew him to her like a bee to a flower. Then didn't let go.

"I've tried a new recipe. I hope you like it," she quickly added.

"Smells wonderful." He stepped back from her, afraid he couldn't keep his hands off her. "I bet you taste better."

She fidgeted with a spoon. He'd gotten away with her. Chad liked that idea.

"How were things at the hospital when you left?" She filled the glasses with iced tea.

"Let's just say I'm glad to be here."

Izzy moved around the small kitchen, and everything about her said home. His chest tightened. He mustn't get used to this. Despite coming out of a bad relationship, Izzy still believed there was a happily-ever-after out there for her. He'd been kicked in the teeth too hard to even think it was possible for him. Would their playing house come back to haunt him?

She turned back to the stove. "We have about ten minutes before dinner. Sit down and talk to me while I finish up."

Chad took one of the two stools at the bar. He checked on Henry, who happily played on the floor. Izzy had already set two places at the bar and brought Henry's high chair over from his house. She thought of everything.

She pulled a casserole out of the oven and placed it on a hot pad between the two plates. Going to the refrigerator, she brought out a bowl of salad and put it on the bar.

"This looks great. I probably wouldn't have eaten and just fallen into bed after a shower if you hadn't invited us over. This is far better."

"I want to see what you think about the chicken recipe." She picked up Henry and put him in the high chair like she'd been doing it forever.

Chad spooned a steaming amount of casserole onto her plate and placed it in her spot, then did the same for his plate.

"I fixed something special for you, Henry." Izzy went to the refrigerator again and brought out a plate with a peanut butter and jelly sandwich on it and a cup of milk.

If he didn't already care for Izzy, she would've grabbed his heart then. "You're amazing, Izzy."

Chad waited to eat until she joined him with Henry in the chair between them. He ate a fork full of food. "This is so good."

He finished his whole plate. "That was wonderful."

"I'll clean up." Izzy moved to stand.

Chad placed a hand on her arm. "Sit. I'll clean up. It's only fair. You cooked."

Half an hour later he sat on the couch with Henry asleep with his head on Izzy's lap. Chad took a seat beside her. He lay his arm across the back of the sofa as he played with Izzy's hair. He couldn't remember a more restful evening. Just what he needed after his day. He had almost let his emotions get away with him over the go-cart patient.

Izzy made the atmosphere easy and comfortable. It felt like a family sharing time together. Everything he had sworn he never wanted again. Even watching a children's movie with Henry asleep had a rightness to it. His fingers teased the circle of Izzy's ear and she shivered. She leaned her head back and smiled at him. Yes, life did feel right. Too much so for his comfort.

The next morning Chad had just finished with a patient and returned to the nurses' desk to do his charting. It was one of the rare times no one was around. He settled in a chair and went to work on his iPad. Something brushed his shoulder. A faint floral scent that could only be Izzy pushed the ever-present smell of antiseptic away.

"How are you doing this morning?" he asked as she came to stand beside him.

Closer than either one of them dared while at work. He'd always been the protector in a relationship. Now Izzy seemed to shield him. "I'm good. You just getting here?"

"Yep. I'm not wild about these half shifts but knowing I'll be seeing you does help."

"What are you up to?"

"I'm just finishing up some charting and thinking about Henry's birthday as it's coming up in a few weeks."

"Do you have any plans?"

He made a face at Izzy as if she'd lost her mind.

She laughed. "Are you confused by the word *plan* or the idea that you should have some?"

Chad quirked the corner of his mouth. "Both?"

Izzy's laugh was that one he loved so much. His thoughts turned to other needs. "If Ms. Weber will take Henry for the night, do you think I could convince you to spend it with me?"

She gave him a coy look. "I don't know. What's in it for me?"

A wicked look filled his eyes. "I'll make it special. I promise."

She looked around, then brushed her hand through his hair. "I'll hold you to that."

It felt good to have someone to tease and laugh with. He'd missed that in his life. Needed it.

With excitement putting an eager step in his walk, Chad went to Izzy's apartment. He'd gotten Henry all settled at Ms. Weber's house already. She'd given him a knowing look and smile, stopping him with a hand on his arm before he left. "Don't you hurt that girl. She's had enough pain and didn't deserve it."

"I don't intend to." Why did he sound so defensive? Was he being unfair to Izzy? Leading her on? Making her believe there could be more between them?

"I know but sometimes we don't think things through like we should. Don't see what we have because we fear a repeat of the past. I'm old enough to know we can change the direction of our lives. Now go and have a good time."

Was he letting his past control his future? Could he make changes in his life?

Not soon enough for him, he finally stood in front of Izzy's door. She took his hand and pulled him inside. Her arms circled his neck.

Izzy kissed him as if she had missed him as much as he had her.

"I've missed you."

Izzy caressed his hair as he nuzzled her neck. "I've missed you more." He walked her back toward the bed. It only took minutes for him to remove her clothes and even less time to remove his own. Their lovemaking was wild and needy. She found her bliss seconds before he howled his release. Wrapping his arms around her, he held her close.

Sometime later he kissed one of her breasts as he sat up. "Next time we'll go slower."

"I didn't hear anyone complaining."

He chuckled. "You do know how to make a man feel good."

"You do the same for this woman."

Chad gave her a tender kiss on the lips. "Mmm… I like that."

He smiled. "I thought we might go out to eat but I like being here just the two of us better. Would you mind if I just order a pizza?"

She kissed his chest just above his heart. "Sounds wonderful to me."

Chad found his pants, pulled them on, then sat on the side of the bed next to her. He placed the call for pizza.

He looked at Izzy, who lay with her head propped on her hand, watching him. The sheet wrapped her body, not revealing anything but everything at the same time. When had he become such a romantic?

His heated gaze met hers as he traced the ridge of her shoulder. "The pizza won't be here for another half an hour." He tugged on the sheet. "I have some ideas about what we can do while we wait. I promise it'll be all about you."

After the pizza arrived, they moved to the bar to eat it. Izzy wore his T-shirt, which looked super sexy on her. It rode up her thighs, leaving a seductive expanse of skin to tease him. Izzy had become a drug he needed. He couldn't get enough of her.

"Chad, can I ask you something?"

His eyes came up. "Sure. You can ask me anything."

"Do Nan's parents know she cheated on you?"

This was one he hadn't expected. "I'm sure they do. She told her mother everything, but we've never discussed it though. With anybody. I don't want Henry to hear negative talk about his mother. I've been careful not to drag Henry's mom's name through the mud. I care about Henry's happiness and his memory of Nan."

"That's admirable of you." Izzy looked at him as if he were the most amazing person she knew.

"Please don't ever say anything to anyone about it."

She laid her hand on his knee. "I would never."

Izzy woke to the sun shining through the large window of her apartment. She reached over to find Chad wasn't in bed, his side of the sheets cool. Opening her eyes, she saw him sitting at the bar with his pants on. His elbows were on his knees and he was holding a mug of steaming liquid in his hands.

Something about him being there seemed so right it made her chest hurt. "Morning. How long have you been up?"

"Just long enough to make us some coffee. I was enjoying watching you."

"You're embarrassing me." She moved to sit on the edge of the bed, bringing the sheet with her. "You are looking rather pensive over there. What's on your mind?"

"I was thinking about Henry's birthday party. That's not really my field of expertise. We didn't do one last year because he was so small and Nan hadn't been gone long. The in-laws keep pushing for one. They want to have it at their place."

She pulled the sheet up under her arms. "If they want to do it, why not let them?"

"Because they keep trying to barge in more and more. I don't think that's what I should be doing. His friends are around here." Chad took another sip of his drink.

"Then plan one. I'm sure Ms. Weber will help. I can help."

Anticipation filled his voice. "Would you?"

"Sure. We could do something here in the backyard. At Henry's age, they're happy with running, swinging and the sandbox. You have all that here. We can add a few games and you have a party."

"You make it sound so easy." A doubtful note hung around his words.

"It's not as difficult as you think. When is his birthday?"

"Two weeks from now."

"Then we better get started." She moved to get off the bed.

Chad put the coffee mug down. "I think it can wait a few more minutes. I don't have you to myself for too much longer."

"You're suggesting—"

"I'm not suggesting." Chad approached the bed, wearing a wicked grin. He captured her as she tried to scramble off the other side, taking her down with him. She giggled as his lips found hers.

* * *

The weeks passed quickly as they planned the party. Chad had had no idea he would enjoy preparing for a child's birthday. Izzy managed to make that fun as well, despite her treating it as if it were a battle and she was the general. When the day arrived, he had no doubt everything would be just right.

They had recruited Ms. Weber, who would prepare the food. He and Izzy had joined her in organizing a menu that would suit the children as well as the adults. Izzy had seen to the ordering of a cake from a bakery that Ms. Weber recommended. The games were all prepared.

Izzy had even spent time filling tiny favor bags even though Chad had questioned if they were necessary. By her look of disdain, he knew he'd gone too far. He'd settled for being the banker and keeping his mouth shut.

By the Saturday of Henry's birthday party, everything was in place. Izzy had him up early, placing tables near her apartment. She and Ms. Weber had decided that Izzy's place would be easiest to work out of for the food. He'd been told to put the grill close by where he would be cooking the hot dogs. The tables all had bright cloths on them. All the chairs in her place and his house had been brought outside. Colorful banners were strung to whatever would hold them.

Henry's plastic pool had been turned into a place to fill up water guns, while another area was roped off for a balloon game. Izzy had thought of everything. He'd never seen her happier. Except for when she'd come for him.

There hadn't been much opportunity for any alone time, but he'd enjoyed every minute they spent together getting ready for the party. Even now as he looked over the transformation of his backyard and Henry running from one spot to the other, Chad couldn't help but take in the changes Izzy had made in their lives.

Izzy came up to stand beside him. "So what do you think?"

He put an arm around her waist and gave her a squeeze. "It's perfect like you."

She returned the hug. "Let's just hope the kids have a good time."

"I'm sure they will. How can they not?" He smiled down at her. "Any chance we can have our own party tonight? The in-laws are coming to the party and taking Henry home with them for the night."

Izzy grinned. "I'll bring the leftover cake."

"I like a woman with an imagination." He moved his brows up and down.

"Then I'll be thinking about what part of your body I want to lick the icing off."

That thought stirred his manhood. "You better behave. I have a children's party to attend, and I might not be presentable."

She giggled. "Got to go. Ms. Weber needs some help."

He grabbed her hand as she stepped away. "Hey, I don't know if I've said thank you for this, but I really appreciate you helping out."

She went up on her toes and kissed his cheek. "You're welcome."

Izzy placed a tray of grilled hot dogs on the serving table near her apartment. She turned toward the drive to see a middle-aged couple in their mid-fifties walking up it. They were fashionably dressed and of medium height.

Were they Nan's parents? Izzy had been looking out for the couple and they were just as Ms. Weber had described them, even down to Mrs. Pritchett having recently lost some weight. They meant nothing to Izzy, but she was still nervous about meeting them. What did they know about her? Had Ms. Weber said something?

As Izzy watched the couple headed straight for Henry. She smiled when they both wrapped Henry in big hugs. Izzy returned to her kitchen and picked up a bowl of chips. To Ms. Weber, Izzy said, "I believe the Pritchetts have arrived."

"Watch out for her. She can be difficult. She doesn't think much of Chad, but he maintains a relationship for Henry's sake."

Half an hour later Izzy helped Chad with the balloon game. The entire time she was aware of Mrs. Pritchett watching her. An air of uneasiness hung around the older woman. Nothing about her looked as if she would be open to talking to Izzy or any other woman Chad might be interested in. If Izzy were in the woman's position, she'd want to know who was having an influence on her grandson.

While the children played, Chad manned the grill. With the help of the other parents, she, Chad and Ms. Weber soon had the children fed. Izzy cut the cake while Chad served ice cream and helped Henry. Izzy led another game, then Henry opened his gifts.

With that done, Chad and Henry told their guests goodbye. Izzy started cleaning up.

"It was a very nice party. I wasn't sure that Chad could pull it off." Mrs. Pritchett stood in front of the table.

Izzy's ears roared with nervousness. "I thought it went well. The children acted as if they had fun."

"They did. By the way, I'm Rona Pritchett. Henry's grandmother. His mother's mother."

"I thought so. I'm sorry I haven't had time to say hello. I'm also sorry to hear about your loss."

It took a few seconds for the woman to speak. "You've been busy. I told Chad we could have this at our house but that's not want he wanted."

It took Izzy a moment to register the venom in her voice. Izzy continued to clean up the table, but her hands trembled. Izzy cleared her throat. "By the way, I'm Elizabeth Lane. It's nice to meet you."

Mrs. Pritchett's eyes narrowed. "So, you are her?"

"I'm not sure who the *her* is you are referring to, but I'm Izzy."

"You're the one Henry talks about all the time." Suspicion filled the older woman's eyes.

Izzy threw some paper plates in the trash. "I hope he says good things."

Mrs. Pritchett's lips pursed. "Exactly how're you involved with Chad?"

"We're coworkers at Atlanta Children's Hospital. He's my landlord and friend." The woman didn't need to know that their relationship had gone beyond that.

Izzy picked up the cake tray, preparing to take it to her kitchen.

"Let me help you." Mrs. Pritchett stepped up to the screen door and held it open.

"Thank you." Izzy moved passed her and into the dim cool area of her home.

Mrs. Pritchett followed her. "I'm asking these questions, because I love Henry. You can understand that I am concerned about the people he is around."

"I've come to know Henry over the last few months, and he's a sweet boy who loves his father and whose father loves him."

"I'm concerned about how you might affect Henry's future. He's lost his mother and may see any woman Chad brings home as his mother."

Izzy sucked in a breath and started for the door. She didn't want to have this conversation with Nan's mother. "Excuse me, I need to see about the food before it goes bad."

"Do you know what Chad has told Henry about Nan?" Mrs. Pritchett glared.

"Nothing but good things to my knowledge. In fact, he wants Henry to remember his mother in a positive light. Chad is concerned about how his and his mother's history might affect Henry in the long run."

Izzy headed out the door. Mrs. Pritchett said, "Chad drove her to have an affair."

One of the nurses from the unit who had a

child Henry's age stood nearby. Had she heard? Chad wouldn't like it if she had.

Izzy quickly gathered the hot dog platter and returned inside. None of this discussion should be public.

Mrs. Pritchett followed her. "You can't trust him."

Izzy put the platter down. "Chad wants Henry to know only love and security. Love from you and from him. I know you're hurting, missing your daughter. But saying hateful things about Henry's father isn't going to gain you anything in the long run."

Tears filled Mrs. Pritchett's eyes.

"I know what you're feeling is part of the grieving process. I'm sure Chad does things in his parenting that you wouldn't do but that doesn't make it wrong. It just makes it different."

A stricken look came over Mrs. Pritchett's face. Minutes went by before she spoke again. "You're in love with Chad, aren't you?"

"How I feel about Chad isn't important. What's important is that Henry feels loved."

"You answered my question. You need to know what you are getting into."

"I already know the type of man Chad is. I've seen him in action at the hospital. He's a compassionate man who cares about others.

I've watched him with Henry. He's a devoted father. He has been a good friend to me."

"What do you think she's getting into Rona?" Chad's low tight tone made Izzy jump.

She hadn't noticed him coming up.

"Izzy rents my apartment. She's a capable nurse in my ER and a good friend who's great with Henry. That's it. Nothing more. That's more explanation than you deserve."

"I have the right to question the woman that might take my Nan's place."

Izzy flinched. She didn't want to replace any woman. She would be her own person.

"That's not going to happen. So you can stop worrying about it. H.G. and Henry are waiting on you. I'll walk you to them."

Over his shoulder Chad gave Izzy a tight smile and took Rona's elbow.

Izzy felt sick. There it was. Chad had said it loud and clear. He had no intention of marrying her. She'd started to hope, to think he might change his mind. They'd been so much like a family over the last few weeks. Chad had seemed happy. She knew she had been.

It was time for that dream to end. She needed to wake up.

CHAPTER NINE

CHAD SHOWERED AND changed before heading to Izzy's. Henry's party had been a success. Thanks to Izzy. The only blight on the day had been Rona. He could see now how much Nan was like her mother.

He'd seen clearly the hurt look on Izzy's face when he had led Rona away. Hopefully he could help Izzy forget what Rona had said. More than once he'd thought about Izzy and icing during the party.

The backyard had been cleared of all things party-related. He'd insisted Ms. Weber go home, telling her that he and Izzy would finish the rest of the cleanup. They had done it without much communication, both focused on what must be done.

Chad knocked before walking into Izzy's place. "Hey, are you as tired as I am?"

"Yeah. But it was a nice party." Izzy sat in the large leather chair.

He walked around her to sit on the sofa. "Thanks to you." He patted the cushion. "You want to come over here and sit by me?"

She looked at him with sad eyes. "I'd better stay here."

His throat tightened. Was this about what Rona had said? "Look, Izzy, you can't pay any attention to Rona. She's always stepping where she shouldn't. I'll have a talk with her."

"Don't do that. It wasn't just her."

"Then what's wrong?" Chad put his hands on his knees. He wanted to pull her into his lap but stopped because something about Izzy's body language said she wouldn't want that.

"It's time for us to call a halt to whatever this is between us."

That was the last thing he'd expected to hear this evening. "Why?"

"I just realized today that I've started to play a game of family and I like it too much. That I would like for it to last but you still don't want that. I've played pretend before. I can't do it again. I'll be moving out as soon as I can find another place to live. I should have known better."

"Why all of a sudden? I thought we had a great day. What happened? Please tell me. Maybe I can fix it."

"I'll tell you, but I don't think you can fix

it." She took a deep breath. "You told Rona that we'd never marry." When he started to speak, she raised a hand. "I've known all along that's how you feel, but I had hoped over the last few weeks you might have started to change your mind. I should have known better. That hadn't worked in my last relationship so there's no reason to believe it should in this one. I had just hoped. It's time to cut it off before it's more painful for all concerned."

"I thought you were happy with the way things are. We agreed to a fling."

"Now the fling is over."

"You don't have to move." The moisture filling her eyes told him this was as difficult for her as it was for him.

"Do you think that I could live out here?" She pointed to the floor. "And watch you and Henry coming and going and pretend there hadn't been something between us. You give me more credit than I deserve."

Panic filled Chad's chest. How had this gone so wrong? He jerked to his feet. "Izzy, you're overreacting. Can't we talk this through?"

"I think we're past that. You need to figure out what you want your life to look like. You must let your guilt go. It takes two to make a relationship. You didn't drive Nan to have an affair. She made a choice. You made choices.

I must make one now. I know what I want my life to look like and I won't settle for less. I had dared to think you might change your mind. Now I know that will never happen. Maybe in time we can be friends."

Chad couldn't push off the hundred-pound weight that had settled on his chest. He snorted. "That's what everyone says, then they never speak to each other again."

Izzy just looked at him.

"I can't change your mind?"

She shook her head.

He headed for the door. "If you decide differently, you know where I am."

A few hours later Chad watched through the kitchen window as Izzy loaded her car with as much as it would hold. A few words thrown out without thought had blown up his entire world.

More than once he started out to ask Izzy not to go. Then he thought to help her load, but he couldn't bring himself to encourage it. He'd hoped she'd get tired and quit. Where was she going anyway? Back to the hotel? Concern tightened his middle.

He sat at the kitchen table, staring at a spot on the wall when there was a knock at the back door.

"Hey." Izzy stepped back so he had to come out of the house. Was she afraid of him? Feared being alone with him in a small space? "I wanted to see if it was all right to keep the key until I get my furniture. Also, I wanted to know if I can stop by tomorrow after work and talk to Henry. It isn't fair to him for me to just disappear. That's scary for a child."

Chad could hardly breathe at the idea of her leaving. With her big heart, she was concerned about how Henry would feel. "Both of those are fine." He paused a moment. "Where're you going? I need to know you're safe."

Izzy was looking at a spot over his shoulder, not meeting his eyes. "Amanda, one of the nurses from the sixth floor asked me the other day if I was still looking for a place. Her roommate moved out for the summer. I'm going there."

"I wish you'd stay here."

"That wouldn't be wise for me or you, and certainly not Henry. Take care of yourself, Chad." She walked toward her car with a stiff back and didn't look back.

He stood in the yard, watching until her little car disappeared. Maybe Izzy was right. He needed to figure out what he wanted. Then he could approach her. And tell her what?

That he wanted to marry her? That he loved her? What? He wasn't sure anymore.

* * *

A long agonizing week later Izzy sat at the unit desk, reviewing charts. She'd lived in a fog of despair since leaving Chad's. Richard had hurt her, but it felt nothing like this bone-deep pain she had over Chad. She'd done the right thing by leaving but that didn't hold her tight in the middle of the night. Or make her laugh. Or make her feel as if she was enough.

She wouldn't be used just because she loved someone. Her head would do the thinking this time, not only her heart. No matter how much it hurt, she would stand up for herself. She wanted, needed more. Yet she couldn't see a happy future without Chad.

During the week she'd stayed out of Chad's way on the days they both worked. Hiding out in her office was really what she'd done. When he passed her, there was no more whistling of "Penny Lane" and only the briefest of eye contact. They were strangers again. Not much better than when they had met at the grocery store. Sadness filled her but she didn't know how to fix their stalemate. The best she could do was plow through each day.

Three loud beeps came over the emergency system radio. "School bus accident," the radio squawked. "Expect major injuries."

Seconds later the ER was like a beehive in full work mode.

Chad came to stand beside her. "What types of injuries are we expecting?"

It was the closest she'd been to him in days. His scent surrounded her. "Broken legs and arms. Head injuries. Possible internal injuries on two."

"I want the internal injuries in exam one and two. I want you with me, Izzy."

She could do this. There were patients to save. She could and would be professional, focused on what she needed to do. Chad and she made a good team. They trusted each other's instincts in an emergency at least. "I understand. I'll go check the rooms and make sure everything is ready." She asked for his ears only. "You going to be okay?"

Chad gave her a curt nod. He didn't look up from the paper he held. "We also need to get another portable X-ray machine down here."

"Already taken care of." She went around the unit desk.

His head rose, his eyes meeting hers. "Thanks, Izzy. I can always depend on you."

She blinked, her chest squeezing.

Fifteen minutes later, under the squeal of the sirens, everybody went into action. The first gurney came though the double doors. Izzy was there ready to show the EMTs where to go. The first patients in were the possible internal injuries.

Izzy pointed to exam one, grabbed the gurney a dark-haired boy of thirteen lay on. She pulled it inside. Chad joined her seconds later. She started gathering vital signs, checking for heart rate and respirations. Chad had whipped off his stethoscope from his neck and was listening to the patient's abdominal sounds. While they did this, other nurses and techs hooked the patient up to monitors.

"We need to get an IV in. Start fluids," Chad ordered. "Along with a full blood panel."

Izzy watched as Chad palpated the child's abdomen.

"Let's get an abdominal X-ray."

Minutes later Chad looked at his tech pad. "Call the OR. Let them know we're sending up a patient with spleen damage. Also, call the blood bank. They need to have A blood standing by."

"I'll take care of it," Izzy said. With that done, she checked on the other nurses, making sure they were handling all the pre-operation orders. "The OR will be ready in ten minutes."

"Come with me," Chad said to Izzy. "Let's check on the other internal injury patient before we start working through the other cases."

Before she left, she instructed the nurses to monitor the patient until the OR staff arrived to get him, then she followed Chad out. They moved into the next exam room where a blonde girl of seventeen waited. They went through the same procedure.

"I need an IV started," Chad stated.

Izzy said, "I'll take care of it." She took the IV starter kit from the tech. After preparing the sight, she efficiently placed the needle. Soon she had the fluids flowing.

Chad continued to examine the girl, pushing on her stomach, checking lower. "We need an X-ray here. The liver is distended. We need to check for damage."

With that patient seen, they went to the next one. Izzy said, "This is a laceration in the hairline."

"I'll need a suture kit." Chad pulled on plastic gloves.

"Already set up for you."

Chad's eyes met hers. "Thanks."

Izzy nodded. They worked seamlessly together. In bed they were perfect, yet an emotional gap as wide as the ocean stood between them.

Working as quickly and flawlessly as they could, they got the most critical patients the care they needed before turning their attention to the less dire ones.

Izzy stayed by Chad's side as they moved from one exam room to the next. The patients went from broken bones down to sprained wrists and knots on the foreheads. Slowly they saw all those injured in the bus crash.

Three hours after they'd started, Chad sank into a chair. He looked exhausted.

Izzy's heart went out to him. She certainly hadn't slept all night since leaving him. "Can I get you something?"

Chad put his head in his hands. "I'm just worn out. I hate auto accidents. And to get a bus load..." He looked at her. "And I haven't been sleeping well."

The sharp edge of being responsible nicked her. Was he implying it was because of her? Yet the knowledge gave her a warm feeling to think he missed her.

"You did a good job today." She wanted to massage his shoulders. Help him somehow. Just to touch him. But she wouldn't. She couldn't open that door. What if she couldn't close it again?

"You did too. We make a good team." He held her gaze with his eyes.

"In an emergency medical situation, we do," she said firmly.

His eyes turned sad. "We're good at more than that. I miss you, Izzy."

She couldn't let Chad sweet-talk her back into his arms. Isn't that what Richard had done? Wanted and needed her for all those things in life where a woman was useful but for what really mattered, she wasn't good enough. Izzy wasn't going down that path again no matter how much her heart ached.

"Chad—"

A nurse stuck her head inside the room. "I hate to say it, Dr. McCain, but you're needed in exam room six."

Chad pushed himself out of the chair. "I got this one, Izzy. If I'm not mistaken, you were supposed to go home hours ago."

He'd kept up with her schedule? In that small way he'd shown he cared. She fought the urge to hug him. Instead she watched him walk down the hall to his next patient.

Chad leaned back in his desk chair. He didn't know how much longer he could take not having Izzy in his life. Not just at work but in his home, at his table, in his bed. He missed her desperately. Just seeing her at the hospital was painful. He ached for her. He'd let his need for her slip two evenings ago when he'd told her how much he missed her. For a moment he'd been prepared to beg her to come back. In the short amount of time she'd been in his and Henry's lives, she'd become important. Vital to their happiness.

Izzy had visited Henry the day after she left just as she had promised. She'd hugged Henry with tears in her eyes. When she explained she had to move and would no longer be in the apartment, one of those tears rolled down her cheek. Henry and Izzy had already created a bond. The boy would recover from Izzy leaving. Chad wasn't sure he would fare as well. Henry asked about Izzy, almost daily. That didn't help ease Chad's pain.

Ms. Weber questioned Izzy's quick departure as well. She'd asked more questions than Chad had been comfortable answering. When her questions ended, she'd started to give lectures on a man who didn't recognize a good woman when he saw one. As the weeks crawled by, they turned into longer lectures. Ms. Weber went on about him taking care of himself so he could take care of others. As subtle or unsubtle as she might have been, the point being he shouldn't have let Izzy go. Chad never offered into the discussion that Izzy had been the one to leave.

The two women had become fast friends while Izzy had been in the apartment, spending time together and having tea while Chad was at the hospital. Izzy had a way of doing that. Making friends quickly.

He pushed his fingers through his hair, then sat up in the chair. Somehow he had to get control of his life. Make a step forward.

Chad's mouth went dry. Sex with Izzy was amazing. Outstanding in fact, but that didn't make marrying her a wise decision. He'd had no intention of ever marrying again until Izzy came along. She had made him wonder what if? Before he wouldn't even entertain the thought of marriage. Now, he cared about Izzy, but marriage?

He ran his hand through his hair. Did he even deserve a second chance? He'd hurt Izzy. Could he be all she deserved? Could he close the door on the ugliness of his past and dare to love again?

He'd messed up big time with Izzy. Had hurt her deeply. If he wanted her back in his life, he would have to prove his love, but he didn't know how to do that. More difficult than that could, he trust Izzy completely?

Enough of those thoughts. He needed to go to the nursing station and sign off on a chart. He pushed out of the chair. As he approached the desk, he could see Izzy on the front side focused on the electronic pad, punching keys occasionally.

Three nurses were huddled close to each other, looking at a picture on the computer screen where they sat behind the desk.

One said, "I can't imagine running around on somebody as gorgeous and nice as he is."

"Yeah, I've always considered him a real catch," another nurse agreed.

Chad smirked. The hospital was a hive of gossip. That's why he didn't want his business known.

"If he was my man, I wouldn't think about having an affair."

The first nurse said, "Yeah, Dr. McCain's all that and a box of chocolates. Imagine his wife running around on him, then he has to deal with her being killed in an automobile accident. How sad it that."

Chad jerked to a stop. His stomach roiled while his jaw tightened and mouth thinned. Those nurses were talking about him. About Nan. His look bore into Izzy's. She'd promised not to tell. Had she been so angry she'd betray him? As Nan had?

Izzy's eyes went wide. Her skin paled as shock covered her face. She shook her head, denying she was the one who had said something. Who else could have? Izzy was the only person he'd told so it must have come from her.

The nurses continued to talk but it was just a buzz in his ears.

Izzy's eyes begged him to believe her.

His heart wanted to believe she hadn't done this to him. His past, the fear and the guilt had him questioning that idea. He'd been lied to before, betrayed. His heart was breaking. He'd thought Izzy was different. Badly he wanted to believe she cared enough about him that she wouldn't take revenge.

He turned and walked back down the hall. Thankfully the nurses hadn't noticed him. How humiliating would that have been? Could Izzy have put an end to their relationship any more efficiently?

He heard Izzy snap, "Don't you ladies have something more useful to be doing besides gossiping?"

That evening in the bedroom of her new apartment, Izzy still felt sickened by what had happened that day. Chad hadn't believed her. He thought she had shared his secret. The look on his face haunted her. She loved him deeply and hated to see him hurt. She couldn't stand the idea she was the cause of his pain.

Apparently the nurse had heard what Rona had said and spread the information. She hadn't missed the accusing look in Chad's eyes. How could Izzy ever convince him she hadn't said anything?

She'd gone looking for him, but he'd been busy with cases. After that, she left a message on his phone, but he'd not returned her call.

Sorrow overwhelmed her. Izzy needed to talk to someone. Her mother. She always made problems seem smaller and answers clearer. Picking up the phone, Izzy punched in her mother's number.

"Mom. It's Izzy."

"What's wrong, honey?"

Izzy hadn't spoken to her parents since she'd move away from Chad's. They had been on a cruise. She hadn't wanted to go into what had happened between her and Chad then, and like now her mother would have known something was wrong just from hearing Izzy's voice.

Izzy had feared completely breaking down then as well as now. She gathered her willpower to hold her emotions in check. She's never been very good at keeping things from her parents, especially her mom.

"Mom, you know I wasn't telling you the truth about how I feel about Chad when we came up to get my furniture."

"Yeah, I know, honey. But after what you've been through, I understood why you spent so much time denying your attraction to him."

Izzy told her what had happened between them. That she had moved out of the apartment and that Chad believed she'd given away his confidence. "Any chance I might have had with him is gone now."

"How do you know? Did he say so?"

"No, but I could tell by the look on his face. He also said he'd never marry me. And after what happened today…" Izzy barely contained a sob.

"He loves you. He may not realize it yet or maybe he's not able to say it. He'll come around. Don't give up on him."

"I don't know."

"Even your dad thinks so. We saw the way he looked at you. Richard never looked at you the way Chad does. You glow when you're around him."

Izzy never thought of herself as someone who glowed. But being around Chad did make her feel warm all over even when they were angry with each other. "I'm not glowing now. I'm miserable. Mom, I don't know how I'm going to go on. I can't keep changing jobs and moving. I have to see him almost every day. But I won't accept less than I deserve ever again. I promised myself I wouldn't settle."

"I'm not disagreeing with that at all, honey. You're a smart woman, Izzy. You'll figure something out. Get him to listen to you. Explain. It could be as simple as just telling him how you feel. Does he know you love him?"

"That's not what he wants to hear. I can't get him to talk to me."

"Keep trying. You have the biggest heart of anybody I know. I think that's what makes you such a good nurse. Chad has that same quality. I'm sure that makes him a good doctor. A good dad, a good man. I don't think I could've ever said that about Richard. I bet Chad's heart is big enough for you too."

"That's not the problem. It's that he's scared to love again. To trust. That won't get better after what happened today."

"You know sometimes when we come out of a bad relationship, we put that relationship off on the next person. I don't think there's much about Chad, if anything, that's like Richard. I doubt there's little or anything about you that's like his ex-wife. Maybe you need to point that out to him, then give him time to figure that out. Think about it."

"Mom, you always put everything into perspective. I love you for it."

"One day you'll have a chance to do the same for your children. You just wait and see. I love you too, honey. Let me know how things go."

Izzy loved Chad as well as Henry. She

couldn't think of anything she wanted more than to be a part of their lives. But she needed Chad to want that too. He would have to figure that out. Right now she wanted him to know she hadn't been disloyal. That he could trust her. With his background, he valued those traits above all others. He had to know she wasn't anything like Nan.

Izzy dropped her phone to the bed. Despite loving Chad as she did, she needed him to feel the same about her. Wanted him to say he loved her. What would it take to make that happen?

Chad walked up to the unit desk the next morning. Everyone was talking at once. He feared it might be about him. Even so he had to face them sometime.

He'd finished his shift in humiliation the day before, then gone home. There he checked his messages and listened to Izzy explain how she hadn't divulged his past. She'd explained about the nurse standing nearby when Rona blurted the affair information out. That Izzy would have never shared his secret.

Minutes after he'd walked away, he'd come to that conclusion. Izzy was nothing like his ex or any other woman for that matter. Loyalty, honor, goodness was ingrained in her. If she cared about a person, she stood by them.

She cared about him and Henry. Never would she hurt them.

He tried to call her to apologize but her phone was busy. He didn't leave a message, intending to call her later. Then Henry had a stomachache and that took up the rest of the evening.

The tech looked up. "Dr. McCain, did you hear? Izzy was in an accident on the way to work this morning."

Chad's heart dropped to his feet. He broke into a sweat. This couldn't be happening, not again. His heart clinched with fear. Was Izzy seriously injured or worse? He couldn't lose Izzy. He loved her.

"Get someone to cover for me. What hospital?"

The tech stammered. "Uh, okay. Downtown Medical."

Five minutes later Chad was in his SUV, driving toward the adult hospital. It was only five miles away, but it might as well have been on the moon for as fast as traffic let him travel. He slammed his hand on the steering wheel when he was caught by another red light.

He'd fought it. Didn't want to believe it. But now when it might be too late to tell her, he could see it clearly. He loved Izzy. He just hoped he had a chance to tell her. To say he wanted her forever.

Chad had convinced himself he and Henry only needed each other, then along came Izzy. She had climbed over the fence around his heart, and under as well, and made herself necessary. Now the stabilizer in his life might be gone. He couldn't live without her.

He'd seen the love between Izzy's parents and what her brother had with his wife. Izzy needed that in her life, deserved it. He couldn't offer her less than all his heart. If he took that chance, it would open the door to being hurt again but Izzy was worth taking the chance.

She was right he hadn't been the only one wrong in his marriage. Nan had shared a part in the failure. With Izzy at his side, he could get beyond his past failures to find a lifelong happiness. He knew that as surely as he knew how to help a patient in an emergency. Izzy wasn't Nan. It wasn't fair to put her inadequacies off on Izzy.

If he lost Izzy, he didn't know what he would do. He loved her more than he could describe. As soon as the light changed, he pushed the gas pedal and roared up the street. A couple of people honked at him as he sped around them.

No wonder she had compared him to the jerk she'd given years of her life to. Chad hadn't offered her any more than Richard had. Their relationship had all been one-sided—in his favor. He couldn't blame her for washing her hands of him. But he intended to change that.

He whipped into the first parking spot he came to, jumped out and ran for the ER entrance. Sliding up to the desk, he huffed out, "I'm Dr. Chad McCain. Is Izzy—Elizabeth Lane here?"

The tech took his painful time checking the computer. "Yes, she's in exam room thirteen."

Chad started toward the double doors.

The tech half stood. "Sir, you can't go back there."

"I'm her personal doctor."

The tech looked bewildered. "Okay."

Chad pushed through the doors. He searched the room numbers until he came to Izzy's. He opened the door. There was no one there. His chest tightened as if a car lay on it. Where was she? Had she died?

He returned to the hall, looking both ways. As he headed toward the nurses' desk, he saw Izzy on a gurney being pushed his way. He hurried to her, taking her hand. "Izzy, where're you hurt?"

"Chad." Izzy gave him a weak smile before her eyes fluttered closed again.

"Thank heavens, you are alive."

"Sir, you need to wait in the waiting room," one of the nurses said.

"I'm Dr. McCain. I'm Ms. Lane's personal physician."

The woman looked down at their hands, then nodded. "Okay, but you need to stay out of the way."

His look didn't leave Izzy when he asked, "How injured is she?"

As they continued to Izzy's room, the nurse said, "Bruised good in several places. The worse is a broken fibula where the other car hit her. That tiny car of hers took the blunt of it, I heard. She has been to X-Ray and should be on her way to the OR in about thirty minutes."

The office staff settled Izzy in the room and left with, "Someone will be in to get her in a few minutes. You can stay until then."

Chad gave Izzy a kiss on the lips. "You scared the life out of me."

Izzy's eyes opened. "I didn't tell them."

"I know, honey. I know."

Soon a couple of people from the OR arrived.

"Izzy, I'll be here when you get back." He squeezed her hand.

"I love you," she muttered.

He kissed her tenderly. "I love you too."

CHAPTER TEN

IZZY'S EYELIDS FLICKERED. She blinked at the blur of something or someone moving back and forth. Where was she? As her vision cleared, she recognized a hospital area. The blur turned into a man. *Chad.*

"Chad, stop. You're making me dizzy."

He came to a jolting halt in his pacing, then moved to the chair situated beside the bed and sank into it. "How're you feeling? Do you hurt anywhere?"

"I'm fine."

He brushed the hair off her forehead. "I'm sorry this happened to you."

She tried to touch his face, but the IV line stopped her. "How do I look?"

"Beautiful."

She smiled weakly. "No, really."

Chad cupped her cheek. "You took a pretty good beating. You're bruised."

Izzy looked around the stark room. "I'm in recovery?"

"Yes."

"They let you back here?" She couldn't believe that.

He dipped his chin and gave her a sheepish grin. "They really didn't have a choice. I called in a few favors."

Chad was really that concerned about her. "You did?"

"Yes." He took her hand, bringing it to his lips. He kissed the back of it. "You scared the hell out of me."

She tried to move.

Chad stood, hovering over her. "Easy. They have your leg all trussed up."

"I can't believe I broke my leg." She looked down at her now-chunky leg.

The worry in her eyes he hadn't expected. "That's much better than I feared."

A nurse approached. "I see you're awake. Are you ready to go to your room?"

"I guess so."

"Let me get one more set of vitals and then I'll send you off." She looked at Chad. "Since you have your own personal physician, you'll be in good hands."

"Yeah, but he works with children and I'm a little bigger than that."

Chad smiled. "I do but the principles are the same."

The next morning Izzy sat in a chair as Chad moved around the room, packing the few belongings she had to take home. The day before he had ordered her nightgowns delivered so she would have something besides a hospital gown to wear. Embarrassing as it was, he'd also helped her during the night to the bathroom. He'd even brought her a large arrangement of flowers when he left for his supper. She couldn't have asked for anyone to be more aware of her needs. He'd called her parents as well and reassured them.

"You know you didn't have to go out and buy me something to wear." She pulled at the full-leg knit pants.

Chad looked at her. "What was the plan? Get those skinny jeans on over that cast?"

She lifted her nose. "Maybe, but I admit there might have been a degree of difficulty." She looked down at her broken leg. "I don't know how I'm going to manage the stairs at my apartment."

"You're not going to. You're coming home with me."

She opened her mouth and Chad held his hand up to stop her. "Listen, then you can argue. Your apartment doesn't have anyone around all the time like my house does. If it's not me, then Ms. Weber is there. If you get in trouble, there's somebody to help you. Come and stay until you're cleared by the doctor and then you can leave. As long as you need a place with no steps, the garage apartment is perfect."

Izzy didn't really have a choice. Chad was right. The apartment would be a better situation if she took it. "I guess so."

Chad's grin was one of a winner. "Don't forget I can offer a tree with a chair under it. With the weather being pretty for another month or so, you'll have a lot of time to enjoy it."

Izzy couldn't deny the appeal. "I do like that idea. But I leave as soon as the leg has healed."

"Good, then it's settled."

Chad drove her to his house and carefully helped her to her apartment, which sparkled with cleanliness.

"I see Ms. Weber has been busy."

"How did you know I didn't do the cleaning?" Chad settled her in the chair and put a pillow under her leg.

"Because as good as you are at most things, cleaning isn't your thing."

His gaze caught hers. "You know me so well. I'm going to get you situated, then go to the house. I'll get our lunch and Henry. He's dying to see you. If you feel up to it."

"I would love to see him. I've missed him." Chad walked to the door. "Chad." He looked at her. "Thanks. You didn't have to do this."

His gaze bored into hers. "Yes, I did. I'm glad I had the chance." He hurried out the door.

What had he meant? *Had the chance?*

Ms. Weber joined them for their meal. When it was over, Izzy yawned. Chad lifted her into his arms while Ms. Weber pulled the bed covers back. Lying her gently down, Chad propped up her leg on a pillow and covered her.

The sun was lowering when she woke.

"Hey there. You want something to eat or drink?" Chad sat on the sofa, reading a book.

"Drink, please." She pushed into a sitting position.

Chad brought her a glass and a couple of pills sitting on the mattress near her.

"Have you been here all the time I was sleeping?" She took the pills and drank all the water.

"I have."

"You don't have to nurse me." She couldn't make more out of that then there was. Chad was a good guy who cared for people naturally.

"I know that. I want to." He moved to stand. She stopped him with a hand on his arm. "I forgot to tell you. I want you to know I didn't tell anyone about what Nan did."

"I know. You told me at the hospital."

"I did?"

"Yes, just before you went into surgery." Chad looked as if he expected her to say more.

"I don't remember anything after the accident until I woke up in the hospital room yesterday afternoon with you pacing."

"Hey, don't make fun of your medical care personnel. He was worried about you." Chad took the glass to the sink. "Hungry?"

"No, thanks. You know you don't have to entertain me."

"I don't mind. Would you like to go outside and watch the sunset?" He came to stand at the end of the bed.

"That does sound nice." Chad scooped her up. "Hey, I can walk."

"Yeah, but I enjoy having a reason to carry you."

Despite the thrill of being cradled against him, she didn't need to think this made things different between them. "Chad, you know this doesn't change anything."

"You need help for a while and I'm providing it, that's all."

For some reason that saddened her.

They watched the sun set and the fireflies come out.

"I think it's time to get you inside and fed." Again, Chad lifted her.

This time she gave no complaint. He sat her at the bar, then warmed a bowl of soup for them.

"Please tell Ms. Weber thank you when you see her."

"Will do."

After their meal, she said, "I think I'll go back to bed. The anesthesia must still be in my system. Plus the pain pills." She started toward the bath with her gown in hand but when she toppled to the side, Chad hurried to support her. He helped her to the bath.

From inside the bath she said, "Dang it."

"What's wrong? Are you okay?" Chad sounded like he was right outside the door.

"I can't get these pants off." She was trying to seat on the commode but there wasn't enough space to straighten her leg.

"Then come out here. I'll help you."

"I'm not going to let you do that."

"Open up or I'll come in. It's not like I haven't seen you before."

Izzy swallowed hard. He had and she'd liked it. Every minute of it. She slipped the gown over her head, then opened the door with her pants still on. Chad assisted her over to the bed, where she laid down. His hand slipped under her gown and pulled on the waistband of her pants. She helped all she could, shimming one way, then the other.

"Izzy," Chad growled. "That's enough of that."

She looked down at him. His eyes burned with desire. He blinked and they returned to all business. Minutes later he had her tucked in bed and all the lights off but a lamp. "Call me if you need me."

"You aren't staying here tonight."

"I am. But don't panic, Izzy. I'm sleeping on the sofa." His words had a tight note to them.

The next four days she was back at home, as Izzy thought of it, went much as the first. Chad took a few days off despite her telling him that wasn't necessary.

"I need to learn to take time off and now is a good opportunity to start."

Izzy looked at him in amazement. Chad really was making some changes.

He and Henry spent most of those days off entertaining her between her naps. Ms. Weber came in the evenings with their meal and joined them.

Her parents made a quick overnight visit. Chad was nice enough to let them stay at his house.

Her mother asked as they sat under the tree, "How're things going?"

"Nothing has changed." Izzy couldn't keep the sadness from her voice.

"But he's taking care of you. He insisted on his call to us he would do it just after the accident. Someone doesn't do that if they don't care."

"That's only because he has a good heart."

Her mother gave her a speculative look, raising her brows. "That's a really big heart. I think it's more."

"He hasn't said anything."

"He will and you need to be ready to listen when he does."

It had been five days since the accident when Chad announced, "I'm going back to work tomorrow. Ms. Weber will check in on you."

"I'll be fine. You've been a great nurse. I appreciate it." Chad had been wonderful to her. Almost as if he did love her. Yet he'd said nothing. The panic on his face in the hospital and the way he stayed beside her as if she were a newborn incapable of anything showed he cared. Still, he didn't mention the future.

Chad moved in a supply of books and puzzles to give her something to do. He'd bought her a learn-to-paint set that he set up in front of the large picture window.

"I thought you could try your hand at painting to pass the time. Maybe do a painting of the oak tree. Since you love it so much."

"You do have high hopes for me." She was touched by the thought Chad had put into keeping her from getting bored.

On the days he was off, he spent a lot of time with her along with Henry. They often sat outside, watching Henry play. Chad had surprised her with a lounge so she could put her leg up.

"You do know you're spoiling me." She had no doubt her heart was in her eyes.

"Which is as it should be." He settled in the chair next to her but didn't look her way.

Was Chad afraid she might see something he didn't want her to?

Soon she could move around the apartment on crutches with little trouble and life formed a pattern. Chad and Henry spent the time they could with her. Their group acted more like a family each day. She looked forward to seeing them. Chad said nothing about the days ahead and neither did she. One afternoon she was asleep on the lounger when the soft touch of lips woke her. She could've sworn she heard Chad say *I love you*, but when she opened her eyes, he wasn't there. Once again she'd imagined it.

She'd been at Chad's three weeks when one

of the nurses from the unit asked her if she'd like to get out for lunch and a chick flick. It was time for Izzy to start pulling away from Chad, become less dependent on him. So she accepted.

Chad looked out the kitchen window for the fourth time in five minutes. It was still early for Izzy to return from the movie. He'd made all the plans for their dinner and for Ms. Weber to have Henry at her house. Now all he had to do was hope.

Chad couldn't take it much longer. He'd stayed away from Izzy, waiting on her to recover from the accident enough to listen to him. More than that, he wanted to show her how he felt about her as well as tell her. He'd spent the last three weeks trying to get to know her better, to make her feel cherished, but it was time to move forward.

He wanted to kiss her, hold her, love her. Tell her how he felt about her.

When had he last been this nervous? Not even when he'd been the head attending for the first time in the Emergency Room. His nerves rattled like a skeleton in the breeze. Tonight had to go well. It just had to.

He wanted a lifetime with Izzy. He needed

to persuade her of that. Convince her he could be what she needed. The man, the lover, the partner she desired and wished for. He had no doubt Izzy was what he needed. The light he'd found when she was near had gone out of his life when she had left. He wanted her warmth forever.

Henry was clean and dressed in his newest pajamas. He and Ms. Weber sat in the living room with her reading to him. Earlier that evening she had helped Chad prepare the meal. He wanted to say he had cooked it. Izzy must feel special. Now the food warmed in the oven in Izzy's apartment.

The backyard was ready. Chad had spent most of the time Izzy had been gone stringing small white icicles lights from the large oak. Under those he'd placed a table for two, then covered it with a white cloth. He'd set the table with Izzy's dishes, not wanting to use the ones he and Nan had shared. He'd added glasses and silverware. Wine waited in a cooler. As a special touch he had bought flowers at the grocery.

He checked the drive one more time. A flash of headlights let him know she had arrived. His heart raced in anticipation as he headed toward the back door. He called to Ms. Weber, "She's here."

Chad groaned. He'd heard the excitement in his voice. He wouldn't let himself think about Izzy no longer wanting him. His heart thumped as he hurried to meet her, helping her out of the car.

He leaned down to speak to Sara, the nurse from the unit. "Hey. Thanks for taking her. I know she's getting tired of my company."

Sara smiled and looked at Izzy. "I doubt that."

Izzy couldn't prevent the blush running up her neck. "He's not too bad to be around. Thanks for thinking of me."

"Not a problem. I enjoyed the movie. Well, got to go."

He and Izzy stood together, watching Sara back out of the drive. Izzy's scent filled his nostrils. She wore a silky blouse and dress pants. Her hair hung free and brushed her shoulders. His fingers twitched to touch it, but he resisted. She looked soft, sweet, feminine and completely desirable. "I didn't expect this welcome." She looked at him up and down. "You look nice."

He'd taken special pains in his dressing even changing shirts three times. He'd settled on a collared fine blue-striped dress shirt, navy slacks and dress shoes. The evening was too important not to look his best.

Her eyes turned worried. "You got a date?"

"I hope so."

Her eyes widened, filled with fear.

"I wondered if you might join me for dinner. We need to talk."

Her eyes brightened and she smiled.

Chad offered his arm. "Please come this way." He led her toward the back door. "Henry wants to say hi before we have dinner."

"I thought he would be having dinner with us."

Chad shifted from one foot to the other. "He decided to accept another invitation. I'm sorry but you'll have to settle for just me."

Her smile made his heart leap. "I don't mind."

"Izzy." Henry came running out the back door with Ms. Weber behind him.

Izzy gathered Henry in her arms, her nose buried in his neck. Chad picked him up, so he was eye level with Izzy.

"Hi, Izzy," Ms. Weber said.

"Hello, Ms. Weber. I wasn't expecting to see you."

"I just stopped by to pick up Henry." She gave Izzy a sly smile. "I better get this one home to bed. Come on, Henry."

Izzy kissed Henry on the cheek. Chad hugged

and kissed him as well. "You be a good boy for Ms. Weber." Chad lowered him to the ground.

Ms. Weber reached out a hand. Henry put his in it. "He'll be fine." She gave each of them a knowing look. "Enjoy your evening."

He and Izzy watched until Ms. Weber and Henry went around the corner of the house.

Chad put out an elbow. "Where were we?"

Izzy looped her hand around his arm, leading her toward her apartment. Her warmth seeped into him. He'd missed her touch.

As they approached the tree, she stopped. Her lips separated in a gasp. "This is beautiful, Chad. Just breathtaking. You did all of this while I was gone? You've been busy."

"I thought you might like it." He led her to the lounger.

She looked around in wonder. "What's this all about?"

"I can't do something nice for you?"

"You've been doing that for weeks, but this is the loveliest of all your ideas."

His chest filled. Izzy liked his efforts. "May I offer you a glass of wine?"

"Yes, please." She settled on the lounge. "This has always been one of my favorite places. It's truly magical now."

Chad opened the wine and poured them both

a glass. He handed one to her with a less than steady hand, then took the chair beside her. A light breeze blew. "You're not too cool, are you?"

"I'm perfect." Izzy looked at him as if memorizing every detail of his face. Her words were soft. "Thanks for all you have done since the accident. I don't know what I would've done without you. You gave me a place to stay and took care of me."

"My pleasure." And it had been.

A gentle smile formed on her lips. Her gaze held his. "You really are a nice guy. You've made me feel very special."

"That's because you are." He cleared his throat. "Are you hungry? Dinner's ready."

She continued to focus on him. "Do you mind if we just sit here for a few minutes?"

He didn't mind anything if he was with her. "Not at all. You just tell me when you're ready."

Izzy took in a fortifying breath. She had to say this. Clear the air. "Chad, I'm sorry I tried to make you be someone you're not. To expect something that you had already said you couldn't give. My only excuse was that I was trying to protect myself. It wasn't fair to you. I'll always regret that."

Chad set his glass down beside his chair,

then moved to sit at the foot of the lounger. He took her drink and placed it beside his. His gaze held hers as he took one of her hands. "I'm sorry too. You had made it clear what you wanted out of life. I listened but I didn't take it into consideration. You deserved better from me. You were right. I needed to quit hiding behind my guilt and my bad marriage. Neither have anything to do with the type of person you are."

"But it wasn't my place to try to make you change."

"You are right. It takes two in a relationship. I might not have been the best husband to Nan, but she made mistakes too. I've been carrying around the idea I'd fail again because I did once without considering things could be different because you're different. Also, I was afraid I couldn't be who you wanted me to be, so I just wasn't going to try. I'm truly sorry for putting the past off on you."

"Chad—"

"Please let me finish." Chad's fingers tightened briefly on hers. "Izzy, we're good together. As partners at work, as friends, as lovers." A note of pain and longing circled his words. "I've never felt as close to anyone. We fit like a lock and key. I don't work without you."

Izzy sat up, trying to get as close to him as she could. Her eyes still held his. "I care about you, appreciate all you have done for me, but I don't see how anything between us can go anywhere." She lifted and dropped a shoulder. "We don't want the same things. I haven't changed my mind about marriage and children. You had that and want no part of that again. I understand. I just think we're setting ourselves up for pain."

Chad straightened. "I think you'd be surprised at what I want. I've thought about what you said. You've changed me, Izzy. Because of you I'm willing to take a chance. I'm trying to set boundaries at work. I now believe that I can be the husband and father that I want to be, or at least I can try if you're beside me. You've shown me what it's like to have someone truly care. For me. About Henry. To be loyal and supportive."

Izzy chest filled with hope.

"When I learned of your accident, I thought I might die." He put her hand over his heart. "I couldn't lose you. You're my life. My heart. My home. I love you."

Izzy stared at Chad. She'd never dared to believe she might hear him talk this way. Her heart swelled. It was almost more than she could take in.

"I told you so at the hospital when you were headed for surgery."

"You did?" She watched him in amazement.

"I did, but apparently the meds had kicked in and you were already out of it."

She sighed. "That I should have remembered. I wish I had. Why haven't you said anything since then?"

"Because I wanted to show you how much I care. I wanted you to feel my love. To see how much I enjoyed us being a family. How much I wanted us to make a life together."

He cupped her face, looking into her eyes. She leaned into his palm. "What I want you to know is that I love you. Deeply and completely. I have for a long time. I just couldn't admit it to myself and certainly not to you. I didn't expect you to come into my life, but you took it like a storm, turning me around and dropping me on my butt.

"You're the best thing that's ever happened to me and Henry. I should've told you that weeks ago, but I was scared. Can you forgive me for hurting you? Will you give me another chance?"

Izzy's heart was almost to the bursting point with joy. She shifted closer. Chad's arm came around her waist as her lips tenderly met his.

Chad took over the kiss, taking it deeper. Her fingers ran through his hair. He pulled her into his lap.

"Mmm…" Izzy pulled her lips away from his. "By the way, in case you're wondering, I love you too."

His mouth found hers again. Sometime later he broke the long hot kiss that had her tingling in anticipation of more.

"By the way, the other day, did you kiss me and tell me while I was sleeping that you loved me?"

Chad smiled. "Which day? I've told you every day for the last three weeks."

Izzy's heart swelled as her eyes turned misty. "Then I need to catch up. I love you with all my heart."

His eyes darkened. "Do you mind if we push dinner back a little while longer?"

"No." She pressed her lips against his brow. Her voice went low and husky. "Why? You have something else you'd rather be doing?"

Chad nudged her off his lap. Standing, he picked her up. "I sure do. If you feel you can handle some activity with that cast on."

"I can if we're careful."

"You don't have to worry about that. I'll always take care of you."

"That sounds perfect to me." She grinned on the way to the apartment when Chad whistled "Penny Lane."

At midnight Chad sat at the table under the oak with Izzy across from him, having finished their warm but dry meal. Earlier they had made love slow and easy, whispering their devotion until they had fallen into blissful sleep.

When they woke up, Izzy had insisted they have their romantic meal. After all, she'd said, Chad had gone to a great deal of trouble to cook for her. Chad had pulled on his pants and she his shirt, then they'd gone outside. He'd seated her at the table, returning inside with a fanfare to fill their plates, while Izzy had refilled their glasses.

"This is excellent." She pointed to the plate.

"Ms. Weber helped me." He filled his fork.

"She helped you plan this, didn't she?"

Izzy rubbed her bare foot over his, sending a stream of desire through him. He wanted to forget about their meal and go back inside. Would she always create this instant need in him? He planned to find out. "Just the meal. The rest was me."

"I've loved it all. I love you." She leaned over to kiss him. "I feel very special."

"You are. I can't promise this all the time. But I can promise to try to make you feel special and loved in some way every day."

Her pleasure at his words glowed in her eyes.

"Would you like to dance?" He stood and offered his hand.

"There's no music." Yet she took his hand.

"I'll hum something." Chad pulled her into his arms. The notes to "Penny Lane" filled the air.

Izzy patted him on the chest. "You and that song."

"You're in my ears and my eyes just like in the song but also in my heart and mind. I love you."

She kissed him as if he were her world. "Back at you."

They swayed a few more minutes before Chad stopped. "There's one more thing I had planned."

"More?" What could be more perfect than tonight?

"Look what I found." He reached behind her.

Izzy turned. Her breath caught. "Chad—"

He went down on a knee. "Izzy, will you marry me? Have children with me? Make my life happy?"

She squealed like Henry in the grocery store and threw her arms around Chad's neck. "Yes, yes, yes. Forever. Yes."

* * * * *

If you enjoyed this story, check out these other great reads from Susan Carlisle

From Florida Fling to Forever
Taming the Hot-Shot Doc
Reunited with Her Daredevil Doc
The Single Dad's Holiday Wish

All available now!